Across the Tracks

Books by Bob and Jan Young

ACROSS THE TRACKS
RUN SHEEP RUN
ONE SMALL VOICE
SUNDAY DREAMER
GOOD-BYE, AMIGOS

ACROSS THE TRACKS

By

Bob and Jan

Young

Julian Messner, New York

Published by Julian Messner
Division of Pocket Books, Inc.
8 West 40th Street, New York

Published simultaneously in Canada
by The Copp Clark Publishing Co. Limited

Fourth Printing, 1965

Printed in the United States of America

Library of Congress Catalog Card No. 58—10924

To all the Betty Ochoas, Dick Ackermans and Pete Flores —that they may build a more understanding and tolerant society than the one we, of the preceding generation, have left to them

Contents

1

The Big Question

"The lever and the fulcrum . . ." Mr. Mead tried to inject a note of challenge into his end-of-the-day voice. "If you'll open your texts, I'll explain tomorrow's assignment."

In the third-floor physics lab of Bellamar Senior High, twenty-two books opened obediently. Only one remained closed. Its owner, a small girl with a slightly up-tilted nose and shiny skullcap of dark curls, bent over her notebook, completely absorbed in the swift, deft strokes of her pencil.

A restless stirring from the front row and Mr. Mead rapped wearily for attention. "I'm sure none of you is more anxious than I for the closing bell." His eyes swept the room, hesitating as they encountered that one small, bent head. "However, I observe at least one person is taking notes. Perhaps the rest of you might profit from Miss Ochoa's example."

At her name, the girl looked up. Her cheeks pinkened. The notebook in front of her contained a curious assortment of sketches: a pirate's head, a triangular pennant, what looked like a huge, floating cloud of balloons . . . Mr. Mead nodded encouragingly. "Now, Betty, if you'll be good enough to read your notes for the benefit of your classmates who haven't been paying attention?"

The girl's cheeks deepened to a rosy crimson as she rose obediently, pretending to study the notebook. "The lever and the fulcrum . . ." she began in a weak voice. On the wall the clock gave a heartening click. The hands leaped ahead two minutes and the welcome sound of the closing bell filled the room.

"Boy, did you ever squeeze out of that one!" Agnes Barnes marveled as the two girls crowded into the doorway. "Haven't you come up with an idea for the dance yet? You've been walking around like a zombie for days." Tall, long-limbed, her freckled face topped by a fiery thatch of curls, Agnes was president of the G.A.A., as well as one of Betty's closest chums.

The small girl glanced up, a faraway look in her eyes, as though even in that freckled face she expected some seed of inspiration. "Not a really good idea. You know what the Decorations Committee suggested this noon? Black and gold crepe paper!" Her pretty nose wrinkled disdainfully. "Crepe-paper streamers . . . they use them for every dance! This is the first event of the year, it has to be special!"

At the foot of the stairs a third girl joined them. If Agnes Barnes' interest was athletics and Betty Ochoa's student activities, one look at Pam Franklin's innocent, doll-like face and fluff of blonde hair told you hers was—boys. But for once, that bubble of excitement in her voice wasn't for date talk.

"Have you heard about the election?" she asked eagerly. "Since Walt Morgan has transferred this semester and won't be Activities Commissioner, Dick Ackerman and Mr. Huxley have decided to call a special election . . . next month when the freshmen choose their class officers."

Agnes nodded. "I'm glad. With almost thirty activity clubs at school, it's a big office. If Dick appointed someone to the vacancy, there'd be screams that he was playing favorites." Eyes suddenly thoughtful, she turned to the small girl beside her. "How about it, Betty? Activities Commissioner ought to be right up your alley. Why don't you run?"

"Huh?" Betty's head jerked absent-mindedly. "I still say crepe-paper streamers are out!" she protested hotly.

The two girls burst into gales of laughter. "Talk about a one-track mind! Old bulldog Betty, with the single-cell brain!" Agnes hooted. But the sting of the teasing was erased by the affectionate hug she gave her friend. A moment later the three of them had swept across the foyer and joined the flow of students going down the front steps.

Bellamar wasn't a new school. One of the few large buildings to come completely unscathed through the disastrous 1933 quake, it had none of the low, sprawling, country-club look of most of the newer California high schools. Compact, three stories tall, those cold cement walls had seemed formidable to Betty as an entering freshman three years ago. She decided that being a senior was what made the difference. Today, the jutting shadow of the

Science wing across the close-barbered lawn, the formal row of stately *cocas plumosas* palms, with their weird tufted tops on either side of the broad entrance walk, even the gray walls themselves seemed strangely softened, familiar, and dear to her heart. Just as teachers like Mr. Mead, friendships, even the weekday routine of classes, club meetings, and after-school Cokes at the Black-and-Gold had become familiar too.

At the boulevard, Pam clapped a sudden hand to her mouth. "Oh, I almost forgot! I'm supposed to pick up an ad for the paper . . . someplace down on Meridian Avenue called El Tipo Café." Her eyes were beseeching. "One of you will come with me, won't you?"

Agnes and Betty exchanged knowing smiles. It was largely through their efforts that Pam had been persuaded to go out for *The Ballast*, the school paper, this year. At least they liked to think it was their efforts rather than *The Ballast's* good-looking editor, "Buz" Manor. The question had been addressed to both girls, but Betty knew it was intended primarily for her.

"Walk six blocks down to Meridian after the workout Coach gave us in fifth period today? Who're you kidding?" Agnes groaned. Before the other two could protest, she was waving good-by, her long legs carrying her up the street. "Save you a couple seats at the Black-and-Gold," she called back wickedly.

Betty and Pam exchanged amused shrugs; then, linking arms, they headed in the opposite direction, toward the south section of town.

Only a few block below the high school, the stores seemed to grow shabbier, smaller. In the windows of some they began to see the first small, lettered placards: "*Se*

Habla Español." Then as they turned onto Meridian Avenue, a broad, one-sided street that faced a weed-grown railroad right-of-way to the south, there was no longer any need for the placards. "*Loncheria,*" "*Abarrotes,*" the words were lettered on the windows of the stores themselves. Fair faces had given way to dark faces, smart fall suits to gay cotton dresses, with here and there an older woman in somber black, an old-fashioned *rebozo* covering her head. They passed two high school girls in tight-fitting black skirts, their pretty faces heavily painted, and their dark hair piled high in exaggerated pompadours. Pam gave no sign of recognition; only Betty managed an embarrassed nod.

Halfway down the block, a gang of boys filled the sidewalk. Tall, broad-shouldered boys like Pete Flores, small, pinch-faced boys like Benny Ruiz; yet somehow they managed to look alike with their dark hair sleeked into identical duck-tail cuts, their ankle-tight peggers and thick-soled shoes. In spite of the September heat, a number wore shiny leather jackets with the head of a grinning white coyote painted on the back.

Betty was aware of the sudden stiffening of Pam's shoulders. Her footsteps slowed. Then several of the boys moved back against the building, making a narrow passage. Their eyes dropped awkwardly to their feet. Only Pete Flores, six feet tall, wavy hair sweeping back from his handsome, arrogant face, continued to stare impudently. Abruptly he flicked away a smoking cigarette, almost between Betty's feet. He called something low and taunting in Spanish.

Pam, unable to understand, passed unscathed, but Betty's cheeks turned crimson. Pete fell in behind them with mocking mincing footsteps. His voice was bolder now. Hearing the burst of snickers from the watching boys, Betty felt the anger rise suddenly inside her, like the mercury in a thermometer that's dipped into boiling water. That Pete Flores! If he thought he could act smart with her!

But before she could swing around with an angry retort, a rattletrap old Chevy pulled up to the curb. A blond boy with a square face and twinkly brown eyes leaned over to open the door. If Dick Ackerman, popular student body president at Bellamar, had noticed the incident he gave no sign. "Anybody going my way?" he asked.

A moment later Betty and Pam, smiling with relief, slid onto the worn seat beside him. "We have to stop at El Tipo, but it's only for a minute," Pam explained coyly. "Afterward you can drop us off at the Black-and-Gold."

Across Pam's head, Dick winked at Betty. "Doesn't even bother to hint, does she? But that's what happens when you're young and gorgeous, and have half the males at Bellamar slavering at your feet." Both Betty and Dick laughed, because this time it was Pam's turn to change a dozen shades of pink.

Inside, El Tipo Café wasn't very different from the Black-and-Gold: a row of narrow booths, a long soda counter, even the same shiny juke box at the very back. Only the music coming from the spinning record wasn't that of a popular dance band, but a plaintive voice in Spanish, emphasized by the rhythmic plunk of a guitar. Ernestina Moreno, a short, stocky woman with a berry-brown face, hurried from behind the counter, wiping her hands on a starched apron.

"Oh, yes, the ad . . . *el aviso*!" she exclaimed in answer to Pam's explanation. Her hands swept broadly. "We have a nice place . . . the high school kids they like, no? We say we serve the Cokes, the ice cream, we keep the clean . . . the very clean kitchen——" In her excitement her voice lapsed into enthusiastic Spanish.

Pam threw Betty a look of sheer panic. Mrs. Moreno stopped to catch her breath. She started over again in English, this time more slowly. Again her exuberance caught up with her and she lapsed into her native tongue.

Betty couldn't control herself any longer. "Look, Señora Moreno, you can't put all those words into one tiny ad," she explained earnestly in Spanish. "We know you keep the clean kitchen . . . everyone knows that. You want a nice ad, something big, something everyone reads and remembers. Here . . ." Betty snatched Pam's notebook. With her pencil she sketched a large square. She filled it in quickly, a few artistic touches, the showy lettering across the top. "Hi, Cats—*Hola Gatos*!" She filled in other words in a catchy slanting line. "Sodas . . . Ice Cream . . . Cokes . . . Tacos . . ."

When she had finished, Ernestina's face was shining. "I like it," she beamed happily. She thrust the paper at Pam. "I like very much. You tell your editor I run this big ad all the year."

'Have any luck?" Dick asked as the girls joined him outside in the car.

"Luck?" Pam echoed, still slightly dazed. "I go in expecting to get a one-inch ad for a couple of weeks. Betty sells her a five-dollar spread for the whole school year! I tell you we're sitting next to a miracle woman."

Across Pam's head, Dick's eyes met Betty's again with a flicker of new interest. "Activities girl, artist . . . don't tell me you're a super-saleslady too?"

A giggle trickled down Betty's throat. "That's me. Jack-of-all-trades, master of none." Only she couldn't conceal her secret pleasure at the obvious compliment. She wished her cheeks weren't getting that funny hot feeling again.

The Black-and-Gold was crowded by the time they arrived. Unable to get a booth, Agnes was holding two chairs at the long center table.

"Am I glad to see you! I'm about to come apart at the joints!" she laughed, swinging her long legs off one of the vacant chairs and snatching a pile of books from the other. "If you only knew what I've been through trying to save these places. I practically had to Indian-wrestle Owen Westbrook!"

From somewhere down the table a husky, good-looking boy in a letter-man's sweater, swung around. "Who's taking my name in vain?"

There were giggles from the girls on either side of him, a willowy blonde named Laurel Wilkie, and a perky redhead, Babs Sutherland. "That's right," Babs put in. "You want to speak of Owen with proper respect. He's going to be our new Activities Commissioner."

"Who says? He hasn't been elected yet!" someone teased.

"Don't worry, chum, I'll be elected. It's as good as in the bag. So far no one's even had the nerve to run against me," Owen's voice was openly boastful.

There was one of those sudden silences that occur in even the noisiest crowds. From the opposite end of the table where he was sitting with friends, Dick's eyes found Betty's. "What do you say, Betty?" he asked. "I bet you could give Owen a race for his money."

For a moment it seemed as though every face was turning to stare at the small girl. Once again Betty was aware of that uneasy embarrassment. What was wrong with her blushing like a twelve-year-old if anyone as much as looked at her! She dipped a straw into her Coke, thankful for the icy coldness against her suddenly parched throat. "Don't count on me. I'm having enough troubles with the decorations for the dance," she alibied.

Even as the words left her lips she knew how lame they sounded. She glanced up. "Besides, I've got to start studying this year. I've made up my mind I'm going to win the art contest this spring . . . or decapitate every one of Miss Potter's best sable brushes trying!"

There were a few laughs, nods of sympathy. Then heads turned back and the question was forgotten in the fresh outburst of chatter. But Betty, silently twirling her straw in her glass, hadn't forgotten. The straw made a little rasping noise as it reached the very bottom.

"Whatever made me say a crazy thing like that?" Betty thought miserably. "That talk about the contest . . . I must have sounded as vain and bragging as Owen. I could at least have left the question open." For suddenly she knew she did want that post as Activities Commissioner. She wanted it so much, it was like a big, aching emptiness inside her. But whether she would run for it—that was a different thing.

2

"What's in a Name?"

It was after five when Betty said good-by to Pam and Agnes in front of the Black-and-Gold. She watched them head uptown toward their homes in Northridge Heights, then she turned down Beach Street, three blocks to its intersection with Paloma Road. In the golden late-afternoon light the tract homes with their gay stucco exteriors, green lawns, and well-kept gardens looked comfortable and beckoning. The house Betty turned into midway down the block was no different from its neighbors, except possibly for the lawn, which was greener, and the flower bed along the driveway, almost overwhelming in its profusion of bright chrysanthemums, geraniums, and late-blooming roses.

As Betty stepped into the pretty living room with its starched crisscross curtains at the windows and friendly chintz-covered furniture, she was aware as always of that warm feeling of home-coming. From the kitchen came the smell of frying beefsteak—not just ordinary steak smell but mingled with the spicy allure of onion, garlic, and chili pepper. In spite of the fact that Betty had been protesting for several months now that she was sick—absolutely sick—of Mexican seasoning, that sudden churning in her stomach made a lie of the statement. Before following her nose and her instincts to the kitchen, she dipped her head into the small alcove off the living room.

The original designer of the house had called the alcove a den, but the Ochoas used it for a combination office and music room. Outside of the green, wall-to-wall carpet, the only furniture was a large desk, which Mr. Ochoa used for the spare-time accounting jobs with which he occasionally added to the family income, and an old but perfectly tuned upright piano. Eleven-year-old Gloria, in sloppy jeans, with her hair in a thick jet braid that hung almost to her waist, was seated at the piano now. Without missing a note of the complicated Czerny exercise, she turned to acknowledge the kiss her sister blew her.

In the kitchen, Betty's mother looked up from where she was equally busy at the big white range. With her velvet-soft eyes and almost top-heavy coil of luxuriant black hair, Mrs. Ochoa was an exact replica of Gloria, twenty years later. Unlike many Latin women, she had not added weight with the years. Betty slipped her arms around a waist as tiny and slim as her own and they exchanged a loving kiss. "And how was school today?" Mrs. Ochoa asked, returning to her stirring.

"Oh, the same as usual. We still haven't come up with the idea for the dance."

Without being asked, Betty went to the cupboard and started taking down the dishes to set the dining room table. Then because here at home she was not used to keeping any secrets, any of the things that were troubling her heart, she set the dishes abruptly on the sink. "They aren't appointing anyone to take Wally Morgan's place as Activities Commissioner. They're going to hold another election. Agnes wants me to run."

Mrs. Ochoa's dark brows drew together momentarily. "And are you?" she asked worriedly.

Betty shook her head. "That's just it . . . I can't decide."

She didn't have to say any more; they both knew what was going through her mind. In the spring Betty had run for President of Girl's League, the office she had wanted all through school. She had been soundly defeated by Babs Sutherland of the exclusive Northridge set. The disappointment had been so great that for the first time in her life Betty had been unable to share it, even here at home with the family. Instead she had made up a lot of pretended nonsense, about how it didn't matter, how she really didn't care. Now Mrs. Ochoa's voice was hesitant. "Maybe this last year you shouldn't run for an office. Maybe you should spend the time at your art work, try to win a scholarship? Just a small scholarship even . . . it would help when it comes time to worry about college."

Betty knew her mother was offering her an escape, a way out so that she wouldn't be hurt again. But instead of feeling a sense of relief, she was suddenly even more miserable, a tight little ball forming in her chest. She picked up the dishes and went into the dining room. Gloria had finished her exercises now. There was the sound of a book being snapped closed, a rustle of sheet music. Then her voice, young and fluid, rang out in the words of her favorite song, "*Corrido Del Norte.*"

That tight little ball flew apart. Betty slammed down the silverware so hard it clattered against the table. "Do you always have to play those crummy Mexican songs!" she exploded. "Can't you sing anything . . . anything American!"

Gloria swung around on the piano bench, dark eyes filling with tears. Eight-year-old Larry, who had just burst through the door, picked up the refrain. "Yeh, ole Mexican songs," he chanted delightedly, "crummy ole songs."

The door to the kitchen opened. "And what is so wrong with Mexican music? What is so wrong with being Mexican?" Mrs. Ochoa's voice was icy with reproof.

The moment the words had left Betty's lips, she had been ashamed. She ran to hug her sister. "I'm sorry, darling," she crooned, cuddling the small dark head. "You sing beautifully. I guess . . . well, I guess it's just that I haven't thought up a theme for the dance. Maybe some dance music would give me more inspiration——"

Gloria's tears vanished as quickly as they had come. She turned back to the piano. Black braid bobbing, she swung into a lively tune that set their feet to tapping.

"Be-bop! Be-bop! That's for me!" Larry did a wild imitation of a jitterbug step. A sudden contortion of his skinny body, and something brown and wiggling popped from his pocket.

"Larry! Larry Ochoa, if I've told you once . . . !" Mrs. Ochoa's voice mingled anger with panic as she sank into a chair and hurriedly pulled her feet off the floor. Across the room, a squealing Betty did the same.

"Gosh, Mom, it's nothing but a little ole alligator lizard!" Larry backed from under the couch, holding the wriggling ten-inch reptile by the neck. "His name's Mickey Mantle. I'm gonna put him in with Pretty Girl . . . maybe they'll have babies."

Mrs. Ochoa had regained her composure now. Her dark eyes sparked. "Not in my house! Not in my house that creature is having babies!" The incident at the piano was forgotten. Laughing, Betty and Gloria watched their mother propel a squirming Larry toward the back door.

From the window over the kitchen sink, Betty's gaze followed them until they disappeared into the small service yard behind the garage where Larry kept the cases for his lizard collection. Before she could turn away, a blue sedan pulled into the drive and her father, smiling and handsome in his gray pin-striped suit, was coming through the garden gate. As had been his custom as long as Betty could remember, Mr. Ochoa greeted her mother first: the warm embrace and kiss that marked eighteen years of happy marriage. Next came Larry, tossed high and shrieking into the air. Gloria, who had heard the sound of the car, raced to the kitchen door. She too sailed high; though for several months now this had required considerable grunting and straining on Mr. Ochoa's part.

Betty was the last, but Manuel Ochoa's eyes were no less tender as he crossed the kitchen to slip his arms around his eldest daughter. "*Chiquita mia,*" he teased, ruffling her hair. "And how is my big girl tonight? Still making things run at Bellamar High?"

Betty's mother looked up sharply, eyes disapproving. "They would have her running things, if they had their way. Another election . . . something called Activities Commissioner. They want her to go through all that again."

If Betty had expected her father to share the obvious disapproval, she was mistaken. "And why shouldn't she run? Why shouldn't she?" he beamed, clapping his daughter on the back. "She's campaigned before. Now she knows the ropes. Everyone knows her name—this time should be easy!"

"Easy!" Betty's knife shredded savagely into the lettuce on the cutting board in front of her. Easy? When your name was Ochoa? When already you could feel it hanging over the school like an ugly, threatening cloud, this trouble brewing between the Mexicans and the Anglos! Hadn't she seen Pete Flores' jeering face this afternoon? Every week the gang of his seemed to grow bigger, those tough, rebellious, hard-faced boys who called themselves "*Los Coyotes.*"

3

Hat in the Ring

"Why, Betty dear, the girls were about to give you up!" It was Mrs. Barnes who opened the door. Even if they hadn't been friends for three years, Betty would have recognized Agnes' mother anywhere: a tall, statuesque woman with carroty hair and a strident voice that matched her daughter's. She was equally familiar with the sprawling, redwood house on Sequoia Circle, with its heavy-beamed ceilings and the myriad French doors and small-paned windows that opened onto vistas of green lawns and sunny gardens.

Mrs. Barnes bobbed her head toward the staircase. "Pam and the Foster girls are already up in Agnes' room. Get yourself some lemonade." Her eyes twinkled. "And you might as well take along the rest of the cookies too."

Without a second invitation Betty headed toward the kitchen, liking the rich, squishy feel of the Oriental rugs beneath her feet. Somehow it never occurred to her to be jealous of Agnes' greater wealth. Maybe it was because both Agnes and her mother wore prosperity well, with a warm friendliness that made everyone welcome.

Betty poured a glass of lemonade from the pitcher in the refrigerator and carefully transferred the remaining brownies from the bakery box on the sink to a bright pottery platter. Agnes' bedroom was on the second floor. Betty's feet in their small, ballet-style flats were muffled by the heavy carpeting. Outside the door she paused for a juggling act, balancing cookies and lemonade while she freed one hand. Then the voices from the other side of the door stopped her.

"It's those Mexicans who are to blame! Mr. Huxley says there's almost four hundred of them at Bellamar this year."

"Oh, they all aren't so bad!" That was Agnes' protesting voice.

"Not bad? They never take part in any school affairs, do they? That Pete Flores and his *Coyotes*, or whatever they call themselves, they've already had a couple of street brawls with some gang from East Los Angeles. They'll make trouble at Bellamar yet, you wait . . ."

Betty fought down a strange, knotted sensation in her stomach, a feeling she hated all the more because deep in her heart she knew it shouldn't be there. She had the knob turned now and with the toe of her flat she pushed open the door. The four girls in gay sweaters and skirts, sprawled on the bed and chairs, looked up with welcoming cries. But not quickly enough to cover that second of embarrassment as Betty handed around the plate of brownies. Selecting two for herself, she sank to the pillow Agnes unceremoniously kicked to the floor and took a sip of lemonade. "Go on, don't let me interrupt."

The embarrassed silence returned. Then with her usual bluntness Agnes waded in. "We were talking about all the new Mexicans at school this year. You know, the ones from Meridian Avenue. Those *pachuco* boys and the girls like Carmen Ortiz, with all that paint and those awful pompadours. Some of them barely speak English. Pam was saying they ought to build another high school across the tracks, a trade school or something . . ."

"I don't think that's such a good idea." For a second Betty had to swallow hard on that knot as she brought out the painful words. "After all, I'm Mexican too."

"Oh, Betts!" Pam's voice was shrill with protest. "You know that isn't true! You're different. You're not Mexican—you're Spanish!"

There was a chorus of eager agreement. Betty was aware of a strange feeling of relief, as if deep in her heart this was what she had wanted them to say. Only Agnes shook her head. "You're all crazy," she charged. "Spanish, Mexican, Dutch, who cares? So Betty's grandmother, or great-grandfather, or someone, came from Mexico. My great-grandmother Schmidt came from Heidelberg, Germany. We're all Americans."

Sybil Foster leaned forward. A thin, angular-faced girl, she would never be called pretty, but her understanding eyes and warm smile were those of the born peacemaker. "So let's all spend a jolly afternoon dissecting each other's ancestry." She yawned, chiding them with gentle sarcasm. Then popping a cookie into her generous mouth and speaking through a resulting dribble of crumbs, she changed the conversation. "What kept you so long, Betty? We about decided you'd fallen into one of Miss Potter's paste pots."

Betty's good humor returned with a giggle at this reference to her favorite art instructor. "Not her paste pots . . . her poster paint and old crepe-paper box, you mean. And the Beaux Arts Club still hasn't come up with a theme for the dance."

Pam stretched lazily on the bed. "I hope you make it something dreamy and romantic——"

"Listen to the glamour gal!" Agnes hooted. "You don't have to be so obvious, darling. We all know you're dying to tell us you've landed a date with the great Buz Manor."

"Well, maybe I have," Pam admitted, turning pink, while the others joined in the laughter.

Agnes looked at Betty. "How about you, anybody lassoed you for the big shindig yet?"

Betty hesitated uncomfortably. She always had a good time at the school dances. Because of her many activities, her easy friendliness, she never lacked partners. But this last year, since so many of the seniors had given up group parties and began pairing off in steady twosomes, dates had become a problem.

Before she could mumble an embarrassed answer, Agnes rushed on. "Well, if not, Dodie, Syb, and I are still unattached too. I thought maybe I'd ask Roger Eaton, Tom Evans, Greg, Butch, some of the kids over here for a snack first—we can all go in a gang."

Betty threw her a quick look of gratitude. "Sounds divine."

"I'll say it does. Am I included?" Pam piped eagerly.

"Invite you? Why should I bother with you? You never have any date problems," Agnes teased. Then seeing the hurt in Pam's eyes, she leaned over to muss her hair playfully. "Of course you're included, if you want to come. But I figured maybe you and the scintillating and debonair editor of *The Ballast* might want to be alone. The way you wander around at school all moony-eyed and wrapped up in each other . . ." A second later the two of them were rolling over on the bed, wrestling and screaming mock insults. Betty and the Foster sisters, exchanging winks, seized the opportunity to help themselves to the three remaining brownies.

It was close to five when Betty said good-by to her friends at the house on Sequoia Circle. She retraced her steps as far as the high school. Except for the white jerseys of the team still practicing on the football field, the huge building seemed deserted. Then spotting a familiar figure turning into Beach Street a block ahead, she let out a cry and broke into an undignified run.

Trim, tailored, in her late twenties, Carla Delgado was attendance clerk at the high school. Though too old to be one of Betty's close friends, Carla lived on the same street, and their mothers were both active in the Altar Society at Saint Gregory's. After the usual polite inquiries about their families, the conversation turned to the dance. "All set with your decorations?" Carla teased.

Betty grimaced. "Hardly! We don't even have a theme and tomorrow's the deadline. I wish I was dead—or at least until next week," she amended hastily. She glanced at Carla. "If Gabriel was still in school, he'd think of something!"

Gabriel was Carla's brother. He had been a brilliant art student, and one of only three in the school's history to win the fabulous Wesley T. Bellamar Art Scholarship. Carla looked down into the eager upturned face. Impulsively she touched Betty's arm. "Gabriel should be home from his last class now. Why don't you stop by the house?"

"You mean it?" Betty gasped, eyes widening. "Oh Carla, I love you . . . just love you!"

Carla laughed. "Here now, stop licking my shoes! I haven't promised anything. He may not be there. Even if he is, he may be too busy studying for one of his college classes."

But Gabriel was home and he wasn't busy. As soon as they turned in the walk, Betty saw him sitting on the porch. A tall boy, thin almost to the point of emaciation, no stretch of the imagination would ever call Gabriel handsome. But something about the broad, high forehead, the intelligent, almost piercing, black eyes, told you that personal charm was the least of Gabriel Delgado's concerns. Even in school he had awed Betty, since he was always aloof and withdrawn into some isolated world of his own genius. She asked about his college work and might never have dared to bring up the dance if Carla hadn't appeared suddenly from the house with two Cokes on a tray and opened the subject for her.

Betty looked at the glasses with dismay, remembering the lemonade and half-dozen cookies she had already eaten. But as the first cool sip slid down her throat, she discovered it tasted good. She began to relax; a moment later she was telling Gabriel her problem. His black eyes were interested. He excused himself and went into the house.

When he returned he was carrying a round cardboard cereal box and some heavy art paper. Betty watched, fascinated. With a few twists of his supple fingers, a couple of snips of the scissors, Gabriel fashioned a handsome replica of a football. Since the dance was to follow the opening game of the football season, that was the logical theme. Instead of the usual overworked balloons of crepe paper, the ceiling of the gymnasium could be massed with cardboard footballs. On the walls they could use bright, easy-to-make posters in the colors of the opposing schools.

Betty looked at Gabriel with growing delight. He wasn't just a "brain"—he was sheer genius. Gabriel's voice, with its soft slur of Spanish accent, hurried on. The decorations could serve a dual purpose. Later in the year the Beaux Arts Club would be asked to decorate the cafeteria for the annual football award dinner. The posters could be reused; this time, with the final game scores lettered in, the footballs could be table decorations.

A half-hour later, with two cardboard footballs balanced precariously on her books, Betty started home. It wasn't just the wonderful idea Gabriel had given her for the dance; talking to him filled her with all sorts of exciting ambitions for her own art career too. Dégas . . . Picasso . . . Betty was certain someday the name of Delgado would be well known too. Ochoa? Well, that would take a little more work.

In all her excitement it was after ten o'clock when Betty realized she had forgotten the afternoon's most important errand. She had forgotten to speak to Agnes about putting up her name for Activities Commissioner before the nominating assembly tomorrow. It was too late to phone now, but she would have to catch her in the halls between classes tomorrow.

Betty didn't find Agnes between classes the following morning. Lunch hour was her first chance to see Miss Potter, the Beaux Arts adviser, about the new plans for the dance decorations. Miss Potter was so enthusiastic about Gabriel's suggestion that by the time Betty finally dragged herself away from the art room, hurried down two flights of stairs and across the quad to the auditorium, the nominating assembly was already under way.

Since the nominations were not of interest to everyone, the huge auditorium was empty except for some seventy-five to a hundred students in the very front rows. Even so, Betty's eyes were unable to find Agnes in the sudden dimness after the midday glare outside. She sank into an aisle seat and opened the brown paper sack with the lunch she had been unable to eat until now. But there was a quivery feeling in her stomach and even her favorite sandwich, tuna with chopped hard-boiled egg and green pepper, failed to look appealing.

The freshmen had completed their business and gone. Owen Westbrook had already been nominated for Activities Commissioner, with Dave Riordan, senior class President, seconding. There was an outburst of talk at the front of the auditorium. Dick Ackerman rapped his gavel for silence.

Babs Sutherland stood and was recognized. She nominated Laurel Wilkie. There was a burst of applause from a tight little crowd of smartly dressed girls in the fourth and fifth rows. A tall, sophisticated-looking girl with harlequin glasses seconded.

Betty folded wax paper around a sandwich with only one bite out of it and put it back in the sack. Her eyes searched the auditorium frantically. Where on earth was Agnes? Once again Dick rapped for quiet. Then it was too still—a long silence that became even longer.

With a sick, hollow feeling in her stomach, Betty realized that Agnes wasn't going to put her name in nomination. It was her own fault. Why should Agnes bother, when she hadn't shown one spark of interest? In a second it would all be over, the nominations closed.

Dick Ackerman looked across the auditorium. "I realize that what I am about to do may be unprecedented, but I believe it is in the best interests of the school. If there are no further nominations, I'll turn the gavel over to the Vice-President." A girl in a green sweater and skirt came forward. Dick descended the steps to the auditorium floor. After a grinning pretense of sitting down, he rose to be recognized. "The chair recognizes Dick Ackerman," the girl in green said.

"With thirty activity clubs at Bellamar, I believe that participation in a single after-school activity, no matter how outstanding, is not sufficient background for Activities Commissioner. I believe the position should go to someone who has taken part in many activities, who has served both as a leader and a worker." Once again Dick's eyes swept the faces around him. "I nominate . . . Betty Ochoa."

There was a moment of stunned silence. Betty gasped, then dove hastily for the paper sack skidding from her lap. Somewhere in the front row Agnes Barnes was on her feet, gesturing frantically. "I second the nomination," she called in her booming voice, without waiting to be recognized from the chair.

There was a small, polite smattering of applause. Betty gathered her books, a couple of folders of brown art paper, her lunch, and walked up to join Owen and Laurel on the stage, thankful that the nominees were not asked to make speeches. Minutes later the assembly was over.

As Betty was leaving the stage, Dick caught up with her. Wordlessly he shifted her bundle of papers and books to his own arms. "I hope you're not going to mind having me for campaign manager—my nominating you without asking you first," he said finally.

Betty still had a dazed feeling, as if she wanted to pinch herself. "Mind? I think it's wonderful!"

"Well, I'm glad that's settled." Dick had a nice grin,

starting with a little quirk at the corner of his lips and spreading to the crinkles around his brown eyes. As they started across the campus, Betty noticed small knots of students turning to stare. Suddenly, for what seemed the first time in her life, she could think of nothing to say. As they crossed the central quad their footsteps echoed hollowly on the cement paving.

The awkward silence lengthened. Betty was aware of a sick, almost desperate feeling. She'd never felt this way before—what was wrong with her? It was as if her mind had suddenly gone blank. In the ell of the big Language-Arts wing, their footsteps reverberated even louder. Abruptly Dick stopped. Balancing the corner of her notebook against the building, he pried open the brown paper sack and peeked inside. "You know, I swear I saw something that looked like a lunch in here," he said hungrily.

Betty's eyes widened. "You mean you haven't had any lunch today either? Do you like tuna sandwiches"—her eyes twinkled impishly—"with hard-boiled eggs and green pepper slices?"

"Tuna sandwiches with hard-boiled egg and green pepper slices—do I like them!" Dick smacked his lips greedily. Suddenly the awkwardness and embarrassment were gone. Betty divided the sandwich, taking the half with the nibble out of it for herself. Carrying both their stacks of books, Dick was still unable to free a hand, and so Betty broke his share into several smaller pieces and, standing on tiptoe, popped them into his mouth as they walked along.

Outside the girl's gym where she had her next class, Dick was finally able to set down the books. Betty divided the rest of the lunch: two chocolate cookies and an apple, which Dick cut in half with his pocket knife. It was only minutes until the bell, but he still made no move to leave.

"You know as your campaign manager, you're going to be seeing a lot of me," he said. "I was thinking we ought to start things off right. How about letting me take you to the game and dance next Friday?"

For a moment Betty's legs felt as if they were turning to sawdust. Dick Ackerman asking her for a date! Dick Ackerman, president of the student body! Last year he had dated Laurel Wilkie; he belonged to the exclusive Northridge crowd. It was Northridge that had put him in office. She wondered if Dick realized what this could mean: a break with his own crowd. But if the thought had occurred to him there was no indication in those friendly eyes smiling into hers. "Well, how about it, favorite candidate?" he asked softly.

Betty wished she could think of some snappy quip, some gay little nothing. Instead, all that came were the simple, direct words from her heart. "I'd love to go with you, Dick."

"Well, it's all settled then," he said and grinned happily.

Betty watched him stride across the campus before she turned and started down the locker-room steps, hoping to meet Agnes and tell her about the date.

Was it her imagination? No, it was true—there was a good inch of pure air between the soles of her flats and the cement steps. First the nomination for Commissioner! Then a date with Dick Ackerman!

4

The Angry One

It was dinnertime, the time for sharing at the Ochoa home. Larry extolled the virtues of his new lizard, a fifteen-incher named Yogi Berra. Gloria said she had been asked to play a piano piece at the school assembly. Finally it was Betty's turn. As she shoved the last bite around and around on her plate, her voice mounted with enthusiasm like a whirling phonograph record, ". . . it's going to be simply colossal! The posters nearly five feet square and so bright they make you blink—the whole ceiling just solid with footballs. Of course, there's the problem of the cereal boxes . . ."

"Cereal boxes?" Mr. Ochoa's mouth dropped. It was

obvious that somewhere in the dizzy pace his daughter had lost him completely.

"Oh, Father, you weren't listening!" Betty pouted with exasperation. "Cereal boxes—oatmeal cartons. We cover them to make footballs. I told every girl in Beaux Arts she had to bring in three or I'd blackball her personally!"

"Betty, really!" Her mother's voice was shocked. "Don't you think you're being a little . . . little dictatorial? Especially now with the election so close?"

"Oh, Mamma, the dance is only four days away. If someone isn't bossy, nothing gets done."

"Betty's right." Mr. Ochoa rose to his daughter's defense. "Sometimes you have to be aggressive to get results." Betty looked down at her plate and thought how right her father was. By not being aggressive she had almost lost that nomination.

Mrs. Ochoa still wasn't convinced but she shrugged with defeat. "You two dynamos—just listening to you makes me tired! I'm glad I'm nothing but a lazy housewife."

Her mother lazy? Betty looked at her mother fondly as she thought of their immaculate home, their well-planned meals, the flower garden that took so much attention, the long hours given to the Altar Society. But even as her eyes filled with a fresh glow of love, she sensed the basic difference between them. For all the modern appliances in her shiny kitchen, for all her smart, up-to-date clothes, Mrs. Ochoa still clung to the old tradition that a woman's life should be bounded by her husband, her family, and her church. She could never quite understand her daughter's driving ambition.

"And how many of these boxes do you need?" Betty's father asked.

"Only a hundred."

"A hundred!" Larry's small face twisted in horror. "Golly, I didn't know anyone liked oatmeal that much! I didn't think everybody in the whole world ate that much oatmeal." It was obvious, from his expression, that the more he pursued the thought the more revolting it became.

"Silly," Betty snapped. "They don't all have to be oatmeal boxes. Salt boxes, Pablum . . . anything, just so they're round."

"And what if you don't get enough?" Mrs. Ochoa asked seriously.

Betty's eyes flashed. "Don't worry, I'll get enough!" Then she grinned, as though ashamed of her own vehemence, and shrugged, "And if I don't . . . well, I'll just think of something else!"

Betty did have to think of something else. By Tuesday afternoon, in spite of the best efforts of the Beaux Arts Club, they were still thirty boxes short. Agnes was playing an important tennis match; Pam had disappeared somewhere with Buz. After school, as Betty started alone down Bellamar Boulevard toward its intersection with Meridian Avenue, she remembered the Sundays last summer when her father had picked up ice cream at El Tipo, packed in large round containers. In her delight over the new ad, Ernestina Moreno ought to donate thirty cartons outright, or at least maybe she wouldn't charge too much for them.

Two blocks below the school, as Betty paused for a street signal, heavy footsteps sounded behind her and a big hand grabbed her arm familiarly. It was Pete Flores. "Hi! Going my way?" he asked in Spanish.

Startled, Betty jerked free from that too-familiar grasp. The last person she wanted to meet was Pete Flores! They had been in one class together, back at Hawes Street Intermediate School, and she saw him occasionally coming out of early Mass, but they had absolutely nothing in common. As the light changed and she started across the street, Pete made no sign of moving ahead. Instead, he shortened his long stride to match hers. "What are you doing down this way? Going slumming on Meridian Avenue?" His voice was taunting.

Betty flushed at the implication. Of all the rude . . . the impossible persons! "Maybe you forget," she told him icily, "I was christened and confirmed at Saint Gregory's on Meridian Avenue. I've been going there every Sunday of my life."

"*Touché!*" Pete tapped his forehead. He grinned impudently, moving closer, his hand trailing along her arm. "Then you won't mind if we walk together, will you?"

Betty did mind. She glanced back furtively toward the high school. If any one of her friends as much as saw her talking to Pete Flores . . . If any of the exclusive Northridge crowd should drive by—even Pam or Agnes—she'd die! Pete was watching her. With a sickening start Betty realized that he had guessed what was going through her mind. What was worse, he was amused. He took out a cigarette, cupped a match to it. "What's wrong, ashamed to walk with me? Afraid some of your rich friends might see you?"

Betty's face turned scarlet. "Of course not! I . . . I was just . . ." her voice trailed away miserably on the lie.

Pete took a long puff on his cigarette. He seemed to be enjoying himself more every minute. "Always polite, always the good little '*wisa*,' " he goaded sarcastically.

Betty winced at that word *wisa*, the *pachuco* slang for "girl friend." Suddenly hot anger surged up in her, scorching her throat. "What's the matter with you? Don't you even know how to talk English yet?" she snapped furiously.

It was Pete's turn to flush. His dark eyes sparked, his

already scowling brows grew tighter. "At least I haven't forgotten how to speak Spanish," he charged bitterly. "I'm not ashamed to be called a *pachuco* . . . a Mexican. I'm not like some people I know, with their rich friends and their fancy airs. I don't have to go around calling myself Spanish!"

The accusation was so sudden, so unfair, that Betty couldn't find an answer. In stony silence they continued to walk side by side. Once Pete's leather-clad arm brushed hers and Betty stole a sidewise glance. Somehow she hadn't realized he was so tall; the top of her head barely reached his shoulder. Even with that outlandish duck-tail haircut he was very handsome, his bronzed face with high cheekbones, his flashing black eyes and curly hair. His arm touched hers again and she was aware of an uneasy, prickling sensation, a feeling that disturbed her all the more because it could be caused by a boy like Pete Flores.

Pete took the cigarette from his mouth and flicked it into the street. At the movement an unruly curl tumbled boyishly across his forehead, and with a start Betty realized that Pete must have been a beautiful child. It was a crazy thought . . . Pete Flores as a baby! But with his symmetrical face and curly hair he must have been beautiful, like her cousin Serafina's little boy, wide-eyed, laughing. What had happened to that little boy to make him grow up so bitter and hateful toward the whole world? She knew instinctively somewhere in his clothing Pete carried an ugly, thin-bladed knife, a knife he had already used in gang fights and would use again. She knew he had been in jail once, interrogated by the police many times. What had happened to that innocent little boy to change him into Pete Flores, leader of the dreaded *Coyotes*?

Aware of the scrutiny, Pete turned. For a moment his

dark eyes were almost friendly. Then like a shadow the bitterness dropped across them. They had reached the door of El Tipo. Pete tossed his hand in farewell. "*Ay te watcho!*" he called scornfully in *pachuco*.

Betty hoped he was wrong—that she wouldn't be seeing him again. As far as she was concerned, she wished she would never see Pete Flores again. Then Ernestina Moreno hurried from behind the counter, her brown face wreathed in welcoming smiles, and Betty forgot all about the unpleasant encounter in her eagerness to explain her errand.

But Betty found that it wasn't as easy to dismiss Pete Flores from her mind as she had expected. Was it her imagination or did he really go out of his way to run into her in the halls at school the next two days? Always, it was when she was with her friends. Each time those taunting dark eyes met hers and he called softly in Spanish, as though they shared some secret. Several times she caught the shocked look that passed between her friends.

Thursday night after dinner Betty was seated at the small desk in her bedroom, trying to catch up with her physics assignments, when Gloria, arms laden with books, shoved through the door. With much giggling, squirming, and rattling of notebook paper she began arranging herself on the bed. Finally, in complete exasperation, Betty looked up. "For heaven's sake! I thought you were going to write your theme at the kitchen table."

"I got put out." Gloria kicked off a saddle shoe with such violence it bounced off the wall. Settling happily on her back, she took off a red bobby sock and examined a blob of peeling nail polish on her big toe. "Mom's got a visitor in the kitchen—Mrs. Flores. And Daddy's using the living room."

"Mrs. Flores!" The lead in Betty's pencil cracked suddenly on the page of her notebook. "Pete Flores' mother . . . What on earth is she doing here?"

"Criminy, how should I know?" Gloria squirmed and twisted on the bed, trying to find a comfortable position. Then her small, dark head popped up and she looked at her sister curiously. "What's it to you anyhow? This Pete your dreamboat or something?"

To her horror Betty found her cheeks turning crimson. "Don't be stupid!" her voice tingled with rage. "That . . . that *pachuco*!" But deep in her heart she knew Gloria had reason to be curious. It wasn't unusual for her mother to entertain visitors. Many of the women in their church sought Mrs. Ochoa's advice, particularly the ones who spoke little English. Often their problems were too trivial to take to Father Gargan himself, but Mrs. Ochoa had been born in the States and was a high school graduate, and could be of assistance. Just because it was Pete's mother . . . what was the matter with her?

An hour later Betty slammed closed her book. Gloria was already undressing for bed. With a squeal of triumph she scooted down the hall to seize the bathroom first. Betty shrugged and headed for the kitchen to get a glass of water.

Outside the door she heard the soft murmur of Spanish. Josephina Flores looked up with a shy smile. She couldn't have been more than ten years older than Betty's mother, but the difference might have been thirty. The lined face was that of an old woman, the hair under the dark *rebozo* totally gray. With her usual graciousness Mrs. Ochoa had spread the table with a bright cloth and the two women were drinking coffee from gay, yellow pottery cups. As Mrs. Flores lifted her cup, Betty noticed her fingers, gnarled and calloused from heavy work. She was aware of a surge of anger at Pete. How many of those lines on his mother's face had he caused, how many of those white hairs were because of his wild episodes? In the Mexican family it was always the woman who carried the brunt . . . little mother of sorrows. Well, that might be all right for the old generation, but if she ever had a son like that, she'd take the strap to him all right . . . and before he became an overgrown delinquent too!

Starting back to her bedroom, Betty heard the faint, distant clicking of the water meter. The bathroom was empty, the door ajar. Her mother must have forgotten the sprinkler running in the front yard.

Outside, the night air had the warm, balmy quality of late summer, a dry, desert-born breeze stirring through the big hydrangea by the porch. As Betty bent to shut off the sprinkler, she caught a pinprick of light under the Chinese elm by the curb. Gradually, as her eyes became accustomed to the darkness, she made out the tall, muscular figure leaning against the tree. It was Pete!

Josephina Flores had been in the house well over an hour. Betty knew the family was too poor to own a car. It was more than a mile from Paloma Road to their small home in the old Mexican section across town. Pete must have walked with his mother all the way and was waiting patiently in the darkness to escort her home again.

Betty was strangely touched. She knew she could pretend she hadn't seen Pete there in the shadows; if he upset her so, she didn't have to speak to him. But with a sudden perverseness, remembering that disturbing feeling she had experienced the other afternoon, she cut across the newly wet lawn toward the elm. "Hi," she called. "I didn't know you were out here. Don't you want to come in?"

There was an arc of light as Pete's cigarette sizzled into

the night. In the darkness he seemed even bigger, handsomer too, as white teeth blazed suddenly against his dark face. "Thanks, but I don't mind waiting," he said softly. There was no bitterness in his voice.

Betty hesitated. "Well . . . well, maybe you're tired of standing then. You can at least come up and sit on the porch steps." Pete fell in behind her as she led the way up the flagstone walk. The two of them sat down on the porch steps. Betty knew she wasn't obliged to stay, but somehow since he refused to come in it seemed impolite to go off and leave him.

"How's school this year?" Betty opened the conversation.

Pete shrugged. "All the same, I guess." His heavy-soled shoe traced an invisible pattern on the bottom step. "I hear you're running for some big office. Think you'll win?"

Betty smiled. "I hope so. At least I'm going to try." She was pleasantly surprised. You couldn't exactly call Pete a conversational giant, but at least he could be agreeable. Abruptly the conversation faded. They sat side by side staring into the velvet darkness.

Pete glanced up at the front door. "She's sure taking a long time."

"I think they're having coffee," Betty explained.

Pete shrugged. "I told her she shouldn't come. I told her your mother wouldn't want to be bothered."

Betty shook her head. "My mother doesn't mind," she said. "She likes helping people."

"Yeah, I bet!" Suddenly Pete's voice had changed, all the anger cascading back. "Yeah, I just bet she likes it." His voice became mimicking and evil. "Poor old Mexican woman . . . poor old soul . . . doesn't know anything . . . doesn't speak English . . . just have to help her!"

The attack, so unexpected and violent, frightened Betty. Then on the heels of fear came anger, hot and suffocating. "What a perfectly horrible thing to say!" she stormed. "I don't suppose it ever occurred to you that maybe my mother likes your mother. That there isn't any pity involved —that she helps her the way one friend helps another because she likes her as a person. You couldn't understand that, could you?"

Betty's voice was as taunting as Pete's had been. "You couldn't understand because you're so busy hating the world, you don't even know what it is to like anybody or anything. You're afraid to like anyone, that's what's wrong with you—you're just plain afraid!"

Even in the darkness she could see the angry red spread across Pete's face. "I am not afraid!" He seized her wrist. "No one says that about Pete Flores. I'm not afraid of anything! I'm mad, that's what!"

In the storm of emotion his hand tightened, biting into the soft flesh of her wrist until it hurt. "I have the right to be mad. Back in Mexico, my father is a big man, *alcalde* . . . mayor of his village. But one year the crops are poor, so my father comes to the States. Does he get work? Does he get a good job? No. In the States he isn't a big man any more, he's just a Mexican. A dumb Mexican. The Mexican doesn't get good jobs—he can dig the ditches, work the railroad gang, clean the streetcars, that's all. He's no good. You know what it's like to have someone call you Spic—dirty Spic—and say there's no work for you? Sure I'm mad, rotten mad!"

"So you take it out by leading *Los Coyotes.* So you lead a gang and get into street fights and you think that shows everyone you are big and important." Betty's voice was scornful.

Pete laughed abruptly, an unpleasant laugh. He jumped to his feet, pulling her with him. "And what about you . . . *Señorita* Betty Ochoa?" he jeered, looking down into her upturned face. "What makes you think we are so different, you and I? This thing that makes me lead *Los Coyotes* and get into fights, maybe it is the same thing that makes you work so hard and run for all those big offices at school? Maybe down inside you remember your name is Ochoa, and you're just trying to show the world you're big and important too!"

As the implication of the words reached her, Betty jerked back. "That isn't true! It isn't!" she protested.

Their raised voices must have carried inside, for the front door opened and Mr. Ochoa, glasses in hand, peered out worriedly. "What's happening out here? Sounds like a dog-and-cat fight. Betty, are you all right?"

For a moment neither Betty nor Pete said anything. Then Pete swung away. "Tell my mother I'll be waiting on the corner," he snapped rudely.

Betty watched him disappear down the walk. Then with a funny, strangled sob in her throat, she brushed past her startled father and ran down the hall to her bedroom.

Gloria was already asleep, arms outstretched in lazy abandon, her heavy braid hanging outside the fluffy down comforter. Gloria with the jet hair, prominent cheekbones, and flashing eyes, who would always look so Latin.

Betty peered intently into the mirror over the dresser. Her hair wasn't black but chocolate brown; a turned-up nose hardly looked Mexican at all. "You'd hardly take me for Mexican.". . . Then as Pete's words rushed back, she threw herself across the bed. "I hate you, Pete Flores," she choked, beating her fists against the pillow. "Hate you, hate you!"

5

Footballs and Confetti

By five o'clock Friday afternoon the last decoration had been tacked in place in the gymnasium. As Betty climbed down from the stepladder, she was grateful for the ice-cream-carton footballs, and gave a sigh of combined satisfaction and relief. Gabriel's idea was more than just good; it was stupendous. Even without the lights, which would not be turned on until dance time, the gym looked impressive.

But the warm feeling of accomplishment was short-lived. As Betty started home along the darkening streets a sudden new misgiving filled her heart. Maybe in the strain of these last days, her mind seemed to have fallen into a permanent worry pattern. This was her mother's afternoon to entertain the Altar Society. What if their sewing project had left the house in a shambles? Betty had never been aware of this concern before; but then, she had never had a date with Dick Ackerman before either. It was important Dick should get the right impression of her home and her family. Everything had to be just perfect. She turned up the familiar flagstone walk, her feet almost flying.

Then as she opened the door and stepped into the living room—soft lamplight casting a rosy glow over freshly polished woodwork, everything in picture-book order, even to the huge, artistic bouquet of mums on the low coffee table—her heart almost capsized with relief. How silly she had been! Her mother had never let her down yet; what had made her think she would fail her now?

There was the scratching noise of footpads on newly polished floors, and Ruffles, the Ochoas' seven-month-old cocker pup, skidded around the door and a butterball of black fur launched into Betty's arms. Mrs. Ochoa poked her head from the kitchen, dark brows drawn together in vexation. "That dog! I thought I locked her out. I knew you wanted things nice . . ."

Betty raised her cheek from Ruffles' soft coat. "Oh, Mamma, everything looks beautiful—just perfect." Her eyes slid from the bouquet on the coffee table to the matching flowers in the dining room. "Even your prize mums. But you were saving those."

"Flowers." Mrs. Ochoa shrugged, dark eyes dancing. "What good are flowers except for something special? And what could be more special than a date with the president of the whole student body?" For a moment Betty had the feeling those dark eyes were seeing right inside her, to every hidden thought, every secret fear. Mrs. Ochoa patted her daughter's shoulder. "Now hurry and get dressed." Again her eyes got that sparkly look. "And don't worry about Gloria either. I told her to throw those awful jeans in the wash and put on a dress for a change."

"Boy, this guy must be a movie star or somepin'!" From the end of the dining table Larry surveyed his eldest sister. Betty had changed into her new red wool jersey with the full skirt; little silver bell earrings dangled at her ears, and around her neck was a matching necklace.

"For heaven's sake, don't be so childish! A student body president is a lot more important than a movie star," Gloria chided with sudden new importance.

Betty's round face, already flushed with excitement, turned even pinker. "Listen, you two," she warned. "You'd better behave tonight. Larry, if you mention lizards just once—Glory, if you have a giggling spell, I'll——" Her voice trailed off without mentioning the consequences, but her tone left no doubt it would be something equal to death by burning oil.

About seven-thirty, Betty answered the doorbell. Dick stood on the front porch. In his tweed sport coat and slacks, with the porch light shining across his blond hair, he looked older than he did at school, more mature. He grinned and glanced at his watch. "Promptness, that's my middle name . . . Richard Promptness Ackerman. Hope I'm not too early?"

Betty laughed. "Heavens no! I've been ready for ages." Then she flushed as she realized the words were a dead give-away as to how anxious she had been. She led Dick inside to meet her family.

He gave Mrs. Ochoa a gracious nod, stepped forward to shake hands with Betty's father. As he sat down on the couch, his eyes dropped to the mums. "What beautiful flowers. I bet they're from your own garden. You ought to tell my mother the secret; she tries so hard, but hers grow all to leaves."

Mrs. Ochoa's eyes sparkled with the compliment. "Maybe she babies them too much," she suggested. "Flowers are like children, you know. They need care and attention, but they can be spoiled too."

Betty looked at her mother in open-mouthed astonishment. What a clever thing to say. Imagine her mother coming up with a charming observation like that! In fact, her whole family was full of surprises. Larry was balanced on the arm of his mother's chair, wide-eyed and alert, without a sign of his usual squirming. Gloria, in a starched pink dress, with her dark hair caught back in a glistening pony tail, was acting like a very proper young lady without even a hint of a giggle. Somewhere deep inside Betty, that last lump of worry dissolved. Why, they were wonderful; she wanted to kiss them all!

When it was time to leave, Dick helped Betty with her coat. They went down the walk to his car. "I like your family," he said as he held the car door. "You know, you're pretty lucky. I always wished I had a brother or sister."

Betty sank back against the seat and watched him turn the ignition key. Dick was right. She was lucky to have such a fine family. Yet it seemed strange, even for a brief second, to feel sorry for Dick Ackerman whose father was an important attorney and one of the wealthiest men in Bellamar.

At the high school they turned into the parking lot, already half filled with cars. Across the street, the huge eyes of the field lights showed above the bleachers, and there was the sound of youthful voices raised in the first school yell:

"B—B—B-E-L
M—M—M-A-R
Bellamar! Buccaneers!"

A moment later they were caught in the crowd pressing toward the gate.

Inside, the lights were almost dazzling as they lighted the green field where the opposing team in blue and white jerseys were already going through their practice routine. Someone yelled from the grandstand. Betty saw Pam, eyes tremulous as she clung to Buz's arm. Others called to them too—Dick's friends, Agnes and the Foster sisters, Miss Potter. As Betty and Dick found two empty seats near the fifty-yard line, she was aware of a small group across the aisle turning to stare. One of the girls was Laurel Wilkie. Betty smiled a friendly greeting. Laurel, eyes frosty, turned away rudely. Babs Sutherland did the same. If Dick caught the snub, he gave no sign. But for just a moment his hand seemed to tighten on Betty's arm. Betty settled onto the bench beside him, two small spots of color glowing in her cheeks. She told herself she wasn't going to let it matter. She wasn't going to care.

Laurel and Babs were whispering to another girl now. All three turned to stare coldly. The two small spots in Betty's cheeks burned brighter. Then Dick grabbed her arm and pulled her to her feet as the home team in black and gold jerseys came running onto the field. Somewhere down in front the band struck up the school fight song.

"*Onward, Onward, Buccaneers.
Forward, Fighting Buccaneers . . .*"

Two hours later, after a 14-to-0 victory over Western High, the excitement spilled from the playing field into the brightly lit gymnasium. The ceiling of bobbing footballs and the gay, poster-trimmed walls were more dramatic than Betty's wildest dreams. Everywhere she heard murmurs of surprised approval.

"Looks like you did yourself proud," Dick teased.

"It wasn't really my idea, it——" Before Betty could give Gabriel credit, they were caught in the jam surging onto the dance floor. A rippling scale from the tenor sax announced the start of the first number. Dick held out his arms.

He was a good dancer. Though Betty's head barely cleared his shoulder, they danced well together. When the number ended they found themselves standing near Pam and Buz. They traded partners. The following number Betty and Buz exchanged again with Agnes and a tall, lanky boy named Roger Eaton.

By now the last stragglers had arrived, and the floor was so crowded that the dancing couples could barely weave among one another. Betty's eyes searched for Dick, but he seemed to have been swallowed completely in the revolving mass of gaily dressed young people. She danced with the freshman brother of one of the girls in Beaux Arts; the boy friend of a girl in her English class. With Miss Potter and two other girls, she made a hasty trip to the cafeteria, through the crisp September darkness, to replenish the punch bowl. When she returned, Mr. Huxley, the principal, asked her for the next dance.

It was a lively jazz number, but he insisted on dancing a sedate two-step that made Betty want to giggle. "To show my complete impartiality, I'm dancing with all the candidates for the coming election," Mr. Huxley informed her. "First the charming Miss Wilkie—now the equally charming Miss Ochoa . . ."

Betty's giggle broke into the open. "What about the charming Owen Westbrook?" she asked.

Mr. Huxley's face remained serious, but behind his heavy-lensed glasses she could see an amused twinkle in his gray eyes. "I shall excuse Mr. Westbrook tonight . . . on the grounds that he has already acquitted himself nobly on the football field," he said sedately. Betty laughed delightedly. No wonder everyone said Mr. Huxley was the best principal Bellamar had ever had. He was fun!

Then as quickly as the laugh had sprung to her lips, it faded. Through a sudden opening in the crowd she caught a glimpse of Dick dancing with Laurel Wilkie, their heads close together. With a sudden change in the rhythm Dick swung his partner around and Betty saw with a strange little feeling of satisfaction that they were quarreling. Dick's face was flushed and angry and Laurel looked on the verge of tears. A moment later the crowd closed in again and they disappeared.

It wasn't until the very last dance that Betty and Dick finally got together again. Even then, as the orchestra struck up the dreamy strains of the final number, she had a moment's misgiving. But suddenly a rugged pair of tweed shoulders shoved through the crowd and above the heads of the others, she saw a long arm waving frantically.

"I was beginning to think I'd lost you for good. Why didn't you warn me I was bringing such a popular partner to the dance?" Dick waited until they had made a half-circle of the floor before he spoke. A smile tugged at the corner of his mouth; those little crinkles branched around his eyes. "But then I should have known. That's what scared me the first time I ever saw you, the way you were always flying around like a whirlwind talking to a dozen people and organizing a half-dozen committees all at once."

Betty missed a step as she stared at him in astonishment. Dick afraid of her? Why, she remembered that freshman year at Bellamar—that bitter first year when she and Dick had seemed to oppose each other on everything. "Afraid of me?" she choked. "What about you? As a freshman, I thought you were an absolute ogre!"

Suddenly they were both laughing as they recalled that freshman year, that seemed so long ago. Betty had been from Hawes Street Intermediate School, Dick from exclusive Northridge. During those first few months at Bellamar the traditional rivalry between the two schools had continued into their freshman activities. "When you walked off with the presidency of the freshman class, I wanted to scratch your eyes out," Betty teased.

"It wasn't much of a victory," Dick admitted ruefully. "If I remember correctly, you were the little number who maneuvered things behind the scenes so that Hawes Street walked off with all the other offices."

"We called Northridge a bunch of snobs because they had all the money. You said Hawes Street was a gang of ruffians because we had the best athletes," Betty reminisced.

Abruptly the music ended. Dick dropped his arms, but his strong hands reached out to engulf Betty's smaller ones. "Well, partner," he kidded, "shall we continue our sparring outside?"

In the parking lot, Dick turned on the car lights. He twisted the dial of the radio until he found the soft music of a dance band. He seemed in no hurry to get started. "You know, that seems a long time ago," he told Betty, his face serious. "Hawes Street . . . Northridge . . . all the petty fighting."

Starting the motor, he backed slowly into the line of cars inching toward the boulevard. "Look at us now. Pam

Franklin, Agnes Barnes, your two closest friends are from Northridge. Over half my pals are from Hawes Street. Somewhere along the way something happened. We forgot about being two separate neighborhoods; we started getting acquainted, working together. I bet half the kids don't even remember those days any more. Now we're one big student body, all pulling together, nobody left out."

Betty looked at the street lights, slipping past like round, suspended moons in the darkness. Dick was right, it did seem a long time ago. Three years ago she never would have dreamed of a date with Dick Ackerman either.

At the corner they slowed for the blinking yellow night signal, and turned onto Meridian Avenue. The small stores were dark except for a single red and green neon sign in front of El Tipo Café. Outside, a half-dozen boys still lounged under the street light—restless boys with duck-tail haircuts, thick-soled shoes, and shiny black leather jackets. Suddenly one of them darted into the street. White teeth drawn into a jeering smile, hands doubled into threatening fists, he tried to stop the car. Dick stepped on the gas and swerved around him easily. But not before a second boy had snatched a rock from the gutter and sent it clattering against the rear fender.

At the next corner Dick slowed again. His eyes met Betty's. He didn't have to say anything; she sensed they were thinking the same thing. One big student body, working together, nobody left out? Who were they kidding? None of those boys had been at the dance tonight. Out of four hundred students of Mexican descent, not more than half a dozen had attended the dance.

6

Black Week End

It was warm for late September, yellow sunshine releasing the sweet, earthy smell of new-mown grass, with only an ocasional breeze rustling through the chrysanthemums to bring a brisk reminder that fall was just around the corner. In identical costumes of rolled jeans and gay striped T-shirts, Betty, Pam, and Agnes stretched on the Ochoas' back lawn indulging in one of their favorite Saturday pastimes: sipping Cokes and reliving the triumphs of the night before.

"The decorations were out of this world," Pam insisted. "Everyone thought so. Why, even Buz said they were pretty novel, and you know Buz."

Betty lifted a cheek from the lawn where she had been enjoying a worm's-eye view of an enlarged blade of grass. She winked at Agnes. It was true that Buz was very good-looking and probably the best editor *The Ballast* had ever had, but he assumed an infuriating air of superiority sometimes.

Agnes sat up, hugging her knees. She winked back. "How was your date with Buz anyhow? I noticed the two of you left the dance early."

Pam flushed an apricot color that made her golden loveliness even more appealing. "Well, maybe we did. But it was such a perfect night, we decided to take a drive . . ." Then as her confusion threatened to become complete, she looked at them in sudden exasperation. "Oh, you two! Always teasing! So Buz and I like each other a lot—so we're going steady now. Is that so terrible?"

"Terrible? Pam, it's wonderful!" Betty reached to give her friend a quick hug.

"Of course it is!" Agnes joined in. "Don't mind my teasing. I'm just jealous." She wrinkled her freckled nose, ran lean fingers through her fiery hair so it stood out in complete disarray. "Now you'd think an absolutely raving, red-haired beauty like me would be able to get somewhere with Roger Eaton—that is, somewhere farther than talking about *gryllus domesticus* or *locustidae*. Bugs! I would have to fall for a guy with his nose so deep in a biology book, the only way I'll ever get to first base is to crawl under a microscope. But at least he's coming over tomorrow to show me his moth collection."

Betty rolled over on her back and pretended to study a jet vapor trail drifting across the sky. Pam's news about going steady with Buz wasn't any surprise. But Agnes being interested in studious Roger Eaton—she didn't know why that should shock her so. Except, that for three whole years now it had been double, triple, mostly whole gang dates that included the Foster sisters too. She felt strangely left out. She thought about last night. Dick hadn't asked her for another date. Of course, she hadn't expected him to . . . really.

A red canvas sneaker poking her shoulder brought her back to reality. "Okay, pal, don't try to run out on us that easily," Agnes goaded. "Everyone else has let down her hair. You know what we're dying to hear. How did you get along with Dick?"

Pam popped up greedily. "Imagine a date with Dick Ackerman! You should have seen Laurel's face when you walked into the stadium. What happened? Will you date him again?"

Betty threw up an arm, pretending to ward off the barrage. "He was very nice. I think I really have a chance now."

"You mean you and Dick might go steady?" Pam's voice was incredulous.

"Silly! Is that all you think about? Not a chance with Dick Ackerman—a chance to win the election!"

"You'll win," Agnes reassured her stoutly. "Sure, Owen is a big splurge around school right now, being co-captain of the football team. And having the lead in the class play last year didn't hurt Laurel any. But as Dick says, Activities Commissioner represents all the organizations, big and little. You already have Beaux Arts. Sybil said they were making posters, your profile in black paper against a white background. Then there's the Spanish Club. I'll line up the G.A.A. and Roger will take care of the Science Club."

"Of course, Owen is one of Buz's best friends," Pam interrupted eagerly. "But he still hasn't made up his mind.

If I can bring him around, you'll get some editorials in *The Ballast.*"

Betty looked up at the sky again; the vapor trail had melted, leaving a clear blue that hurt her eyes. It was a wonderful feeling, knowing she had loyal friends. Even more wonderful was that other feeling she'd had since last night. She knew Dick was partly responsible, but everyone had been so friendly at the dance that for the first time she really felt she could win this election. The pleasant thought was interrupted as Gloria stuck a cheery face out the back door to call her sister to the phone.

When Betty returned, she wondered why the others didn't notice the difference immediately, the way her feet almost melted down the back steps in that fluid motion. But Pam and Agnes were deep in conversation. Agnes glanced up. "You know, spending Sunday looking at a moth collection doesn't appeal to me exactly. Maybe I could ask Roger to get Tom or one of the other fellows and we could go bowling."

Betty plucked at a blade of grass; she wished she didn't blush so easily. "It sounds nice, but I'm afraid I can't make it. That call was from Dick . . . we have a date for the show."

At the looks of stunned amazement she shrugged casually. "Oh, it's nothing big. We're just going over plans for the campaign." But the dancing excitement in her eyes belied the pretended nonchalance.

If weekdays followed a routine in the Ochoa home, Sundays had their special pattern too. Since Sunday morning was Mr. Ochoa's one chance to sleep, the family always attended late Mass at Saint Gregory's. Afterward, Mrs. Ochoa, Betty, and Gloria rushed home and changed from church clothes to cotton dresses to put the finishing touches on the turkey or the ham, the chili beans, enchilladas, or the hot little meat pies called *emplanadas,* which they served their guests. Sundays there were always guests: friends, relatives, godparents. By two o'clock in the afternoon there would be one or two cars in the driveway, maybe another at the curb. What was left of the food would be pushed back on the stove to wait for still others who might come later.

This Sunday there was Cousin Serafina, her husband and little boy; Larry's godfather, Dr. Romero, and his family. Later in the afternoon Uncle Jaime with his five children and tiny, frail Grandmother Ortega arrived from East Los Angeles. As always, the men gravitated toward the back yard to talk business, while the women headed for the kitchen to drink endless cups of dark coffee and discuss babies, patterns, and new curtains. Usually Betty loved these reunions. She and Gloria herded the younger children onto the front lawn, where they organized games, or into the den, where Gloria played the piano and they all sang. But today there was none of her bubbling enthusiasm. She carefully avoided taking the children onto the front lawn; even in the den, her voice didn't quite match the others in the singing.

From time to time her eyes strayed to the front window. Why didn't some of them leave? How could she introduce Dick to all this crowd? She wished suddenly that her grandmother spoke better English, that Uncle Jaime didn't have such a huge, booming laugh and that way of slapping everyone on the back so that their teeth joggled. Then she was ashamed of herself, because she loved them both dearly.

By five o'clock the Romeros had gone, but Uncle Jaime's ancient sedan and Serafina's newer coupe still stood in the driveway. As a familiar robin's-egg-blue Chevy pulled to the curb, Betty choked back the small lump of misery. It was too late now. Dick was already here.

Before she could reach for her coat, her mother appeared in the archway. Mrs. Ochoa's eyes swept across the heads of the seven children noisily playing Bingo now, little Jorge's face smeared with chili sauce, Larry and one of the twins pummeling each other. "I think your young man is here," she announced as though she, too, had been watching the street. "I think maybe tonight it will be all right with your father if you meet him outside."

Betty threw her mother a look of undying gratitude and wriggled into her coat. From the kitchen came Grandmother Ortega's thin, querulous voice in Spanish. "Rita. Who is it? Rita, you aren't letting that child go out without a chaperone?"

"Hurry. Hurry!" Mrs. Ochoa whispered, shoving Betty out the door with only the hastiest kiss on the tip of her upturned nose. "You leave *Grandmacita* to me."

Smiling with relief, Betty raced down the front walk. And sometimes she thought Mamma was strict and old-fashioned! Suddenly she wondered what it must have been like when her mother was a girl, with Grandmother Ortega who thought no proper young man and young woman should be seen together until after they were married?

Dick met her at the sidewalk. His eyes swept the cars. "What's going on—a party?"

"Oh no," Betty explained. "Just family."

Dick blinked. "I thought I met them all."

Betty held up her hand. "First family, yes. But these are relatives: grandmother, uncle, aunt, cousins . . ." Then as she ran out of fingers to count, she laughed. "Mamma thought maybe you'd rather not meet them all."

Dick joined in the laughter. "Well, we might miss the

show and I think I've timed it just right so we'll make the second feature."

He was right. They arrived at the theater just as the second feature was starting. Sitting in the close darkness, Betty was aware of Dick's arm resting casually beside hers. Once in a particularly exciting scene, when it seemed certain the hero couldn't possibly escape from the trap the secret agents had set for him, Dick reached over and gave her hand a little squeeze. The intermission lights came on and part of the audience filed out. After that came the main feature. For the next hour and a half Betty forgot all about Dick in the laughter that bubbled up inside her at the antics of her favorite comedy team.

It was close to nine o'clock, the streets dark, when they came out of the theater. Dick suggested a hamburger at the Black-and-Gold. On a Sunday night, without the tables crowded with teen-agers, the hangout seemed unfamiliar: no activity, no din of after-school chatter and laughter, just a few couples talking in subdued voices. Dick led the way to a booth. They ate their hamburgers: golden toasted buns, crisp meat, and succulent tomato slices, in complete silence. That was one of the nice things about being young, Betty decided. You could gorge yourself on ham and *emplanadas* and a few hours later still eat a hamburger with all the gusto of absolute starvation.

"Well, I think we've both added a pound or two," Dick said when they topped the snack off with a couple of thick chocolate malts.

"Horrors, I hope not!" Betty grimaced. "On you it's all right. But a few more pounds and I'll be as wide as I am tall."

Dick's eyes twinkled. "That still wouldn't be very big. Anyhow, you look just right to me."

Betty's heart warmed with the compliment, even though she knew she had fished for it. Suddenly the conversation, dropped so unceremoniously with the arrival of the hamburgers, zoomed forward again, a happy, relaxed conversation full of little surprises. Like going to the juke box and discovering that they both had the same favorite tune, that they both preferred basketball to football, deep-South jazz to the current rock and roll. Dick told Betty he hoped to be a mechanical engineer when he got out of school, though his father was still holding out for a second lawyer in the family. "What are you going to do after graduation, or haven't you made up your mind?" he asked.

"Oh, I'll be an artist, I guess." Betty traced a design on the shiny tabletop.

"Are you any good?"

The bluntness of the question startled her for a moment. Then her dark eyes sparked. "Well, I think I am. I won third place in the contest last spring. This year I'm going to try for first. Of course, if I'm elected Activities Commissioner, I may not have much time . . ."

"*If* you're elected!" Dick snorted. "You're going to be elected. What do you think I'm doing—just wasting my time?" Then both of them laughed as they realized they had already wasted almost an hour when they should have been making campaign plans.

Dick, his face now serious, leaned across the table as he outlined the schedule. Both Laurel's and Owen's campaign managers were introducing them in the home rooms on Monday. He was saving Betty until Thursday. That way, she would appear alone without the competition of another speaker, and her name would be remembered longer. However, at the big student assembly, he was maneuvering for first position. Even though the speeches were limited to three minutes, sometimes the audience became bored. Betty bobbed her head; it sounded like good strategy.

Plans completed, she saw with dismay that it was almost eleven o'clock—a whole hour after she had promised to be home! As they turned onto Paloma Road, Betty saw that her house lights were ablaze. The cars were gone from the driveway now. There was a sudden skidding sensation in her chest. Father was so very particular. Were they waiting up for her? Then the front door burst open. Without even glancing at the couple pulling up to the curb, Mr. Ochoa raced down the steps and around to the garage. Betty stiffened. They weren't watching for her. Something had happened. Something was wrong!

Dick pounded up the steps just behind her, through the front door that was standing ajar. Gloria, big-eyed, huddled on the living room couch. Just around the corner in the alcove, Mrs. Ochoa was talking on the phone. "Yes, Father Gargan. I'm on my way now."

She laid back the receiver and turned to face them, cheeks drained of color. "I'm going to the Delgados'. Gabriel is dead. Killed in a gang fight an hour ago!"

Betty sank weakly to the couch beside Gloria. Gabriel dead? *Los Coyotes!* But it couldn't be true—Gabriel had never belonged to any gang in his life!

7

Spic!

Overdone bacon, underdone eggs, Larry's ears that needed washing, Gloria's hair that had developed a hopeless tangle: Betty had never realized quite how much her mother was the hub of the family until this morning.

Mr. Ochoa was little help as he sat morosely over a cup of weak coffee, reading the paper. He had already been down to the newsstand to pick up the last edition. It was all there for the world to read, how Gabriel returning from an art lecture in the city had been killed by a bullet from a homemade "zip gun" as he got off the bus in front of El Tipo Café. The police believed the assailants were members of the notorious "*Calle Nueve*" gang from Los

Angeles, who had mistaken Gabriel for a member of *Los Coyotes,* with whom they had been feuding lately. Gabriel . . . who could have been another Picasso.

Betty turned with a start to snatch the coffee pot that was bubbling over. Gloria still hadn't gotten the snarl out of her hair. Larry couldn't find his third reader. Then over the confusion came the peal of the telephone.

"*Chiquita mia?*" Betty almost sobbed with relief at the sound of her mother's warm, efficient voice. Larry's reader was in the drawer of the desk—the cold meat in the refrigerator was for the children's sandwiches—Mr. Ochoa and Betty were to buy their lunches today, there was extra money in the little pitcher on the top shelf. She reported that all was well at the Delgados'. Mrs. Delgado had suffered a mild spell with her heart, but she and Carla were being brave. However, Betty was to deliver a message to Mr. Huxley that Carla would not be back to her job at school for a few days. As Betty hung up the phone, it was with the miraculous feeling that, tragedy or not, somehow their world had been righted again.

By seven-thirty Mr. Ochoa had left for work. At eight Gloria and Larry, freshly scrubbed and with full lunch sacks, were on their way too, and Betty locked the house behind her. Across the street, blackbirds were pecking industriously on a newly watered lawn and old Mrs. Harrison was hanging out her wash. For a moment it was almost possible to believe that last night had been nothing more than an ugly nightmare.

But the news of the tragedy had already reached school. As Betty turned up the cement walk she was aware of a new charged atmosphere, students gathered in little knots, talking excitedly. She passed a group of gangly boys in black letterman's sweaters. "It's all those Mexicans!" she heard an angry voice. At the foot of the steps a tall, sophisticated-looking girl was talking. "Not safe to walk the streets . . . my Dad says they ought to push them back across the tracks, all of them!" Head high, with color flaming in her cheeks, Betty brushed past them and up the steps to deliver her message in the principal's office.

First period was home room. As Dick had predicted, Laurel and Owen appeared with their campaign managers. Laurel's was the usual platform—a promise to work her hardest, promote good feeling between the different organizations. She was such a pretty girl, with her caramel-blonde hair and heart-shaped face, there was a generous round of applause.

Even before Dave Riordan stepped forward to introduce his candidate, the applause started again. It wasn't surprising; they were both well known, Dave as senior class president, Owen as co-captain of the football team.

Owen's speech wasn't the usual campaign fare. Even as the handsome football player stepped forward, Betty was aware of the change, that electric feeling filling the room. "I think we can dispense with the usual promises about doing a good job, working hard for the clubs"—Owen grinned mockingly—"I think I've proved I can work hard and do a good job too . . . at least on the football field."

Everyone laughed. Owen's face sobered and he motioned for silence. "All right now, we've had our fun. I think it's time we talked about something more important, something that happened just last night. Gabriel Delgado was a pretty swell guy. Gabriel was a brilliant guy, a genius, I guess you'd call him . . ." As Owen went into his eulogy of Gabriel's achievements, Betty could feel the class pulling with him, falling under the spell of his voice.

Owen stepped forward, crashing his fist into his palm.

"But Gabriel's dead today—dead because of a certain element we have in this school. Who's going to be next? You? Me? We don't need a lot of talks about clubs working together—what we need in this town is another school! That's my platform: Another high school across the tracks! Let these troublemakers go to their own school, and we'll go to ours!" As his voice ended, it was like a wave breaking over the class, shouts, applause, stamping feet.

Betty sat stunned, her stomach knotting, for a moment afraid she would be sick. There were few students from Meridian Avenue at school today. The Mexican colony was in mourning; the Delgados were dearly loved. But in the front row Jenny Lopez, with her smooth black hair, stared down at her desk, not a flicker of emotion on her small, pointed face. In the back Benny Ruiz sat with that same stony composure, only the brilliant crimson spreading up his neck betraying his emotion. The two of them . . . No, the three of them—Betty looked down at her own tightly clenched hands—were the only ones who had not joined the applause.

"But they couldn't mean these terrible things! They really couldn't feel that way!" a small, protesting voice cried inside her. Had Owen forgotten that there were many families of Mexican descent who no longer lived in the old section across the tracks—that there were many third-generation people like herself—that even among the second and first generation there was only a tiny handful who took part in gang activities? Had Owen forgotten that Gabriel himself had been of Mexican descent?

At noon Betty caught Dick in the cafeteria, just as he was coming through the check stand. They found a small table where they could be alone. "People will say you're chasing me, woman," Dick teased as he unloaded his tray.

"Oh, that popular Dick Ackerman, that devastating, effervescent personality . . ."

But there was no answering grin on Betty's face. It was hard to begin. "Dick, I had to see you alone." She hesitated. Her throat was dry and tight-feeling. "Dick, I've decided not to run for Activities Commissioner . . . I want you to withdraw my name."

"What?" Dick choked and his spoon clattered to the table. "You can't drop out now, Betty. Whatever gave you this crazy idea?"

Betty's cheeks grew pink. "You know why."

"No, I don't!" Dick's eyes flashed, his voice was angry.

He certainly wasn't making it easy. Betty stared down at the table. "It's because of what happened last night, Owen's speech this morning, the way everyone feels . . ." It was hard to bring the words past that constricting tightness. "You know, Dick, I'm Mexican too."

For just a second Dick's eyes seemed to soften, but not those angry lines around his mouth. "So your name is Ochoa. Do you think that makes a real difference? Sure, everyone is upset today and that hothead Owen has stirred up a lot of hysterics. But it won't last a week." He leaned forward intently. "Look, Betty, every student in this school knows that *Los Coyotes* had nothing to do with Gabriel's death. It was some gang from out of town. But any school that could kindle so quickly against the innocent kids in its midst has a real problem on its hands. That's why you have to win this election. We need you on the Student Council this year."

Betty continued to stare at the table. Suddenly she was ashamed of her cowardice, of the disappointment in Dick's eyes. She wished for a moment she could tell him how she really felt. She didn't belong with the kids from Meridian

Avenue—Pete Flores had made that clear. For all her friendship with Agnes and Pam and her work in student activities, trouble started and she didn't belong with them either. Neither fish nor fowl. Suddenly, overnight, she was just Betty-in-between, balancing all alone on a high fence not knowing which way to jump.

"Naturally you're upset now, your family is so close to the Delgados. But think it over for a few days," Dick pleaded.

"I don't have to think it over, Dick." Betty's voice was humble. "Of course I'll stay in the race. I guess I've been acting pretty silly."

"Not silly—human." Dick's face crumpled into a smile of relief. He handed her something across the table. "Here, I bet you haven't eaten yet today. If I remember correctly I still owe you half a lunch."

Betty looked down at the salad in front of her. For the first time that day the familiar giggle bubbled up in her throat. "Tuna . . . with hard-boiled egg and green pepper slices!"

Betty took a bite of the salad. As her eyes met Dick's, they exchanged a wink. She knew she wasn't going to let him down. Maybe after today she didn't have much chance for the election. But together they were going to put up a fight—a fight Bellamar would remember for a long time.

True to Dick's prophecy, by mid-week the school had quieted down. On Wednesday morning Betty was excused for a few hours to attend the requiem Mass for Gabriel at Saint Gregory's. She was surprised to see so many familiar faces: Mr. Huxley, looking faintly embarrassed because he was not familiar with the Catholic ceremony, Miss Potter, who had managed to slip away from her art classes, Pete Flores and the other members of *Los Coyotes,* strangely solemn in their dark Sunday suits. Betty was over the first shock of Gabriel's death now. After all, she had known him only slightly. All that was left was sorrow for his family, regret that one so talented should have died so young.

On Thursday, accompanied by Dick, Betty made her speeches in home rooms. She knew she looked her best: her good black and red plaid skirt, the new bulky red wool sweater Grandmother Ortega had knit for her. Her simple speech, urging better understanding between organizations and races at Bellamar, was well received. In each room there was a generous smattering of applause, though it never reached the fevered pitch that had greeted Owen's oratory earlier in the week.

However, the speech must have carried more weight than they thought. The following Monday, Laurel dropped out of the race, throwing all her votes to Owen Westbrook. Never a heavy runner, Laurel had controlled only a few hundred votes at best. But they were votes Betty would not receive. Dick refused to be discouraged. "So we lost a few votes." He shrugged. "We'll pick them up Friday."

"Well, Gloria could bring up a delegation from grammar school and Larry could round up his Cub Scouts." It was hard to make jokes when you wanted something so badly it had become a big ache inside you. But Betty was rewarded by a flash of admiration in Dick's eyes.

Thursday was the day before the election. Betty was late arriving at school, having stopped to help her mother hang out some of the mountainous wash that had accumulated during her recent stay with the Delgados'. As she bounded up the front steps Betty saw a crowd of students milling around one of the posters in the main hall. Suddenly the door to the principal's office opened. Face purple with anger, Mr. Huxley strode across the hall and elbowed his way through the crowd. He tore the poster from the wall, crumpling it in his fist. At the same instant Agnes darted from the crowd and tore down a similar poster on the opposite wall. But not before Betty had seen.

They were her posters, the cute posters made for her by Beaux Arts with her round face and perky upturned nose silhouetted in black. Only they weren't cute or clever any more. Across them someone had chalked in bold letters a single ugly word: SPIC! BETTY OCHOA—SPIC.

Betty steadied herself against the wall. For a second it was impossible to stem the hot rush of tears. When she realized that she had been recognized, pride swept to her rescue. Head high, she brushed past the students and on down the hall to her first class. Eyes followed her, some curious, some embarrassed. But none, not even the friendly ones, could reach her. None could share the pain, that feeling of desolate loneliness.

Dazed, Betty sat through the next hour of senior English, her fingers taking notes mechanically. She was thankful when Mrs. Miller, with understanding eyes, passed her by for oral recitation. Who could have done such a thing? Who could have been so cruel?

She thought of Pete and of how she had taunted him about being mad at the world. She was ashamed of those taunts now. For the first time she realized a little of how Pete felt. For the first time she felt it too—that terrible, destroying anger, as if she wanted to smash something or send a book crashing through the window.

When the bell rang, Betty was the last one to gather her books. She was in no hurry to leave the room and face the others in the hall. Even the thought of joining Pam and Agnes had lost its flavor.

When she finally came through the door, the main corridor was bustling with activity. Betty gasped as she saw a huge poster newly tacked on the opposite wall, a hurriedly lettered poster on brown paper. DICK ACKERMAN FOR BETTY OCHOA. Next to it was a smaller poster on white paper. AGNES BARNES FOR BETTY OCHOA. Beyond, there were others. PAM FRANKLIN FOR BETTY OCHOA. ROGER EATON FOR BETTY OCHOA.

In one hour the corridors had been transformed. Everywhere posters were blossoming as students scurried back and forth tearing pages from their notebooks, corners from their lunch sacks. Small scraps of paper, notebook paper, drawing paper—crayoned posters, inked posters, penciled posters. It had become a craze, sweeping the school like wildfire. It was Dick's answer to the slander, the answer of a lot of fair-minded students to an attack that had been both vicious and unprovoked.

Even as Betty watched, she saw a tall, raw-boned girl whom she had never met in her life tear a page from her notebook. The girl scribbled something, then looking around to make sure no teacher was watching, she popped a wad of gum from her mouth and stuck the paper to the wall: MABEL ALLBRIGHT FOR BETTY OCHOA.

Mr. Huxley came out of his office. There were strict rules at Bellamar governing campaign posters and defacing the walls, just so much space being given to each candidate. But if the principal saw the illegal banners, he gave no sign. For a moment Betty even thought she saw a hidden twinkle behind those thick glasses.

"Well, how do you like it, kid?" Agnes slipped an arm around Betty's waist.

"Oh, Agnes, I don't know what to say . . ." Betty stopped. Then she was hugging Agnes so hard it left them both gasping. After that there was Pam, Sybil, and Dodie too.

"Say, if this is a loving match, let me in. Just step right up, ladies, and throw your arms around this trim, thirty-two-inch waist . . ." It was Dick, teasing as always.

Betty would have liked to hug him too, but all she could do was sputter all over again. "Dick, I don't know what to say . . . Dick, I . . ."

His big hand shot out to rumple her dark curls. "Forget it, pal. They asked for a fight and we're giving it to them."

Forget it? Betty knew suddenly that even if she didn't win the election, she would always remember this day. As long as she lived, this would be a day to remember.

It was late when Betty got away from the art room that afternoon. She had stopped to talk to Miss Potter for a few minutes about the refreshments for the next Beaux Arts meeting. She knew there was no use looking for Agnes or Pam. Agnes had a hockey game, and if Pam wasn't busy down in *The Ballast* office, she would be somewhere with Buz. As Betty came down the front steps she was almost relieved to see that the wide cement walk was deserted. It was good to be alone for a minute after such an exciting day. Then, as she reached the sidewalk along Beach Street, she saw something brown fluttering against a telephone pole.

She stepped closer. It was another poster, a brown lunch sack with crudely traced letters. PETE FLORES FOR BETTY OCHOA. PACHUCOS FOR OCHOA. Betty choked back a strange lump in her throat. She didn't know whether to laugh or cry. How typical of Pete! Of course, it would never occur to him that his endorsement could completely ruin her campaign!

8

We Won!

Gloria stood in front of the dresser mirror, pouting thoughtfully as she held first a yellow then a green ribbon against her dark hair. Neither matched the exact shade of the oversized chartreuse sweater she was wearing. She hesitated; then opening a top drawer, she rummaged through a neat pile of silk scarfs until she came up with one of the identical shade.

"What are you doing?" Betty bristled into the room, her voice scratchy with anger. It was hard to tell if the rosy color in her face was from outrage or the heat of her recent shower. "I thought I told you to stay out of my things . . . isn't it enough you're wearing my sweater already?"

Gloria's dark eyes clouded with hurt. "But this is the day I'm to play the piano in assembly. You promised I could wear your sweater——"

"Well, I didn't say you could help yourself to everything!" Betty crossed the room and slammed the drawer noisily. "Just look at the mess you made!"

Eyes shiny with tears, Gloria swung around and stamped out of the room, but not before Betty heard her parting mutter. "Old crab . . . mean old crab."

Betty's hands knotted and she stifled a hot retort. Sometimes she wondered just why she had to have younger sisters and brothers! Five minutes ago it had been Larry. Imagine bathing a water turtle in the washbasin at seven in the morning! Now it was Gloria, going through her things as if she owned them! She had every right to be furious.

Her eyes found her reflection in the mirror: brows pulled together so they formed two dark exclamation marks above her nose, her usually sunny mouth stretched into a thin line like a rubber band. The image was so grim that it became ridiculous. Her hands relaxed. Impulsively she stuck out her tongue. "Gloria's right: you are an old crab!" she scolded. "Just because you're wound up like a kinked light cord, it's no reason to blow a fuse!"

Five minutes later, dressed in her black skirt and gray sweater, with a gay red scarf knotted at her throat, Betty joined the family in the sunny kitchen. Only Gloria, nursing her hurt, refused to look up.

"I'm sorry, honey." Shamefaced, Betty shoved the chartreuse scarf across the table. "You can wear it . . . you can keep it if you like."

"Oh, golly—oh, thanks!" Gloria's nimble fingers were already looping the scarf around her black pony tail. But even the instant and forgiving smile she threw her older sister wasn't enough to untie all those knots in Betty's chest.

Twice, moving back and forth between stove and table, Mrs. Ochoa let a hand trail along her oldest daughter's shoulder. Her mother didn't have to say anything. Betty knew the message behind that loving hand, those softly worried eyes. She shouldn't let it matter so much. She shouldn't let it be so important. But how could she help caring? This was the big day. By three o'clock this afternoon the election would have been decided.

Shortly before eight an auto horn sounded out in front. It was Agnes in her mother's big, late-model sedan, borrowed especially for the occasion. "We can't have you walking to school today," she explained as Betty scrambled in beside her, spilling books over the glistening new seat covers. "Today you're going to be delivered in style."

"The famous last ride," Betty quipped. "Maybe it would have been better if you had borrowed Turner & Watson's black hearse." Agnes laughed. But a moment later, as the car filled with silence, Betty realized the joke had not come off too well. Intent on her driving, Agnes didn't turn her head. "Feeling nervous?" her voice was almost too casual.

"Who . . . me?" Betty sputtered, tossing her dark curls. "Don't be silly. It isn't *that* important." It was a lie. Suddenly even with Agnes—Agnes who was her very best friend—she was unable to share her true feelings. How could she tell anyone how important winning this election had become . . . if she didn't win she wouldn't even want to go on living.

First hour, English; second hour, history; third, Spanish. . . . At the eleven-fifteen early lunch period, as Betty came out of the Language building, she saw that the voting booths had already been set up in the big center quad and the first lines of students were forming to get their ballots.

Agnes and Pam were waiting in the usual spot under a small acacia tree on the senior lawn. Today, it was the two of them who kept up the companionable chatter as they ate their lunches. It was all Betty could do to force out an occasional comment, and even the homemade fudge that Pam passed around had the strange texture of caked sawdust. Then Agnes gathered up their sacks and papers and shoved them into the shiny green receptacle. "Well, we might as well get in line . . . three votes for Ochoa coming up."

At the edge of the quad, Betty left the others to take her place in the line marked O to R. After signing the register and receiving her ballot, she waited for an empty booth. She was surprised when the curtains parted and Carmen Ortiz came out. She had never known Carmen to show an interest in student activities before. Then Betty was alone in the cramped privacy of the small cubicle.

Since this was a special election the ballot was brief—the office of Activities Commissioner, a minor vacancy for assistant cheer leader, a proposition to change the name of the yearbook from *Skull and Crossbones* to the more dignified *Pirate's Log*. As Betty inked the small "x" next to her name, a crazy thought pricked at her mind. What if this was her only vote? What if the results were some two thousand votes for Owen Westbrook and only one for Betty Ochoa? Then, grinning at her own idiotic imagination, she completed the ballot and came out into the bright sunlight where Pam and Agnes were waiting.

After lunch came physical education. In the excitement of a rousing volleyball game and the relaxation of the needle-prick shower afterward, Betty was almost able to forget her tension. But an hour later, as she came up the locker-room steps, she saw a gang of husky boys taking down the voting booths and carrying the tables back into the basement cafeteria. The lower classmen who had the late lunch period had finished their voting too. It was all over now. Somewhere up in the student offices the Election Committee was already counting the ballots.

Fifth-period art was Betty's favorite class. Since it was Friday and most of the students had completed their week's project, Miss Potter took this afternoon to discuss the annual art contest. All students in the regular art class were invited to compete—first prize was a fifty-dollar government bond, with lesser prizes of ten and five dollars for second and third. The paintings would be on display at the Beaux Arts booth during the spring carnival. With the exception of the first-place winner, which remained in the school's permanent collection, all entries could be marked for sale, one-half of the money going to the student, the other half to Beaux Arts.

Miss Potter held up some of the previous winners, stepping occasionally to the window for a better angle of light. They were remarkably good. Betty knew she would have to work very hard if she expected to win. Though Miss Potter did not give the names of the artists, there were two she recognized immediately from their bold, almost flamboyant style as having been done by Gabriel Delgado. Both the technique and in that peculiar, arresting quality that marks a truly fine picture, they were far above any of the others. But it was the water colors that drew most of Betty's attention. After all, it had been her small water color of a beach scene that had won third prize last year. Only this year she had to come up with something much better, something really outstanding.

That was it, she told herself firmly. If she lost the election today, she would really throw herself into her art work. She'd start right now working on her entry for the contest. Maybe if she worked hard enough she might even win a scholarship. How crazy she had been to let the election become the center of her whole life!

A half-hour later a blank sheet of paper still stared at Betty from her drawing board. Two crumpled and rejected sheets lay in the wastebasket beside her. This just hadn't been her day for inspiration. She hadn't come up with one single, usable idea. . . . Already the others around her were putting away their supplies.

The door opened and a girl in a Kelly green skirt came into the room. For a moment Miss Potter bent over the paper the girl handed her. Then, removing her glasses, she rapped sharply on her desk. "Attention, students! I know you all have been waiting for the results of the election. The office has just sent the final returns. For Activities Commissioner: Owen Westbrook, 978 votes; Betty Ochoa, 1,162 . . ."

The rest of the results were lost on Betty's dazed ears. Sybil Foster, wiping her hands on a paint-stained smock, rushed forward to seize her in an ecstatic hug. Others around her were popping up, grinning, and calling congratulations. Betty beamed at them all, loving them all, wanting to burst into a million pieces of pure, shrieking joy. She'd done it! She'd won!

Of course Betty knew she hadn't done it alone. After that first giddy moment she had time to calm down a little. Dick, Agnes, Pam, all her loyal friends in Beaux Arts and the Spanish Club—they were the ones who had done it for her. But still it was hard to sit through that last hour of the day in the physics lab. The moment the final bell sounded she was out the door racing down the stairs.

The offices were filled with students, victorious candidates, managers, well-wishing friends, the new freshman class officers, their young faces bursting with pride; the tall, gangly boy with a comical face who was the new cheerleader. Somehow Betty elbowed through the jam to where Dick Ackerman, propped against his corner desk, was talking to Buz Manor.

Dick turned, eyes lighting. "Well, candidate, I told you you'd make it. What do you say now?"

"I don't know what to say . . ." Betty stammered. "I'm so happy. It was a close race wasn't it, Owen gave me a terrific time of it?"

"Two hundred votes," Dick laughed. "But that was enough."

Betty gave Buz a brief statement for the paper, thanking those who had voted for her and promising to do her hardest. By the time he had gone, some of the crowd had thinned out. She and Dick were able to talk without shouting. "You're the one I have to thank the most, Dick," Betty told him. "You're the one who really deserves the credit—you kept me going."

Dick smiled. "I did my best, Betty. But don't thank me. If you want to thank someone, thank Pete Flores."

"Pete Flores?" Betty could feel her mouth dropping.

"Didn't you notice? Where were you today?" Dick shook his head wonderingly. "For the first time in Bellamar's history the Mexican-American students turned out for an election. I think every one of them voted. There's no way to tell, Betty. But that's four hundred votes . . . four hundred votes that could have made the difference."

Betty looked around the office at the laughing, jubilant faces. Not one was the face of a Mexican-American. Yet from somewhere four hundred students had come forward to make their voices known today—students who had never bothered to vote before.

She turned back to Dick. Suddenly she had that feeling she had experienced many times before, that the two of them were thinking exactly the same thing. It wasn't just a matter of personal victory. If four hundred students could be reached to take part in an election, four hundred students could be reached again to take part in other activities. "I won't let them down, Dick," she promised soberly.

"*We* won't let them down," he corrected.

Then as Betty was starting for the door, his voice reached after her. "Hey, I almost forgot. I'm giving a little party at my house tonight—a victory celebration. Someone will pick you up about seven-thirty."

It was impossible to be heard over a new rush of freshmen pouring through the door. But Betty bobbed her head happily; standing on tiptoe, she raised two fingers in a victory salute. What a day this had been! What an absolutely marvelous, out-of-this-world day!

9

Price of Victory

If there had been a thrill in receiving the congratulations of her classmates at school, perhaps the happiest part of Betty's victory was sharing it that night at home with her family. As though some small voice had foretold the success, Mrs. Ochoa had prepared a special dinner: baked salmon, well garnished with garlic and Spanish sauce, the small *pan de dulce,* or sweet rolls, which were Betty's particular favorites.

As Betty's voice mounted faster and faster on that turntable of excitement, she still remembered to give Dick and Pete credit for their assistance. "Honest, all I did was make a few speeches. Dick and Pete were the ones who got out the votes."

"This Dick and Pete!" Mrs. Ochoa sniffed disdainfully, but there was a hidden twinkle in her eyes. "You would think they were eight feet tall! Maybe you could give your own mother a little credit too. Didn't I speak to all the ladies in the Altar Society . . . and Father Gargan too, reminding him he might very well put in a good word where it would help?"

Betty winked at her father, then both of them were laughing. It was hard to imagine Betty's shy mother accosting the rather formidable Father Gargan; but the determination in her voice left no doubt but what she had. "Oh, Mamma, you're wonderful!" Betty flew around the table to seize her mother in an octopus hug.

It was a full minute before Mrs. Ochoa was able to free herself from those eager arms, but her face was rosy with pleasure. "Just remember, success is always a family affair," she told her daughter.

Betty knew she was right. They had all shared in her victory: Papa, whose hearty optimism had given her courage; Mamma, working quietly behind the scenes; even Larry and Gloria—who had put up with her miserable temper these last few days. How she loved them all!

But the celebration had its solemn moment too when her father handed her a gift. As Betty pulled off the wrappings, she saw a new red leather binder, her name in shiny gold letters across the top. "Oh, it's beautiful!" Her fingers traced the velvety surface, already loving the rich, expensive feel. "It's for the notes of my new office . . . the Activity and Student Council meetings, isn't it?"

Mr. Ochoa nodded. "Winning an election is just the beginning. The important thing now is what you will do with it."

Betty knew her father was throwing her a challenge. By

the end of the year what kind of notes would fill this binder? The halfhearted scribblings of just another glory-conscious office-seeker? Or would it be filled with new ideas, with the results of hard, honest work that would make both her family and her school proud of her?

Promptly at seven-thirty the doorbell rang. It was Agnes, her carroty hair a flaming halo in the glow of the porch light. There was a last-minute scramble as Betty rushed for her coat and Mrs. Ochoa locked the small overnight case. Since this was a special occasion, she had given Betty permission to spend the night with her friend.

When the two girls reached the sedan at the curb, Betty was surprised to see Roger behind the wheel and Pam, Buz, and the Foster sisters jammed into the back seat. She hadn't realized that Dick was inviting so many. Five minutes later, as they turned into the driveway of the big white colonial house on exclusive Ridge Road, her misgivings increased. She had passed the Ackerman home many times but had never been inside before. Now, with all the downstairs lights ablaze and the big circular drive already lined with parked cars, it looked even more imposing.

Babs Sutherland opened the front door; behind her was Dave Riordan. As Babs showed the girls where to put their wraps in the little powder room off the entrance hall, Betty caught a glimpse through an arched doorway into the living room. The rugs had been rolled back and a dozen couples were dancing, among them Laurel Wilkie and Owen Westbrook. How typical of Dick that he should include the vanquished as well as the victors!

In the powder room, Betty joined Pam for a last-minute inspection of her lipstick. Agnes, unmindful of such necessities, sank onto a chintz-covered chair and stretched her long legs. "Some house . . . and did you catch that mob outside? Good old democratic Dick."

"I think it was nice of him," Betty answered primly. But the words weren't exactly true. She wished there hadn't been so many people. And that luscious green taffeta dress Laurel was wearing. Why hadn't she worn her new red velveteen instead of this simple gray wool?

When the girls came out of the powder room, they found that the boys had drifted away, leaving only Roger. His homely, bony face was embarrassed as he glanced at them. Then stepping forward gallantly, he offered his arm to Betty first. "May I have the pleasure of this dance?"

Pam and Betty couldn't help giggling at his solemn air, even though Agnes threw them a withering look. Then Dave Riordan swooped between them. "Sorry, old man," he told Roger. "Dick's orders. He wants Betty in the playroom right away." As Betty trailed Dave down the hall, she was aware of Roger and Agnes moving onto the dance floor, while from somewhere Buz had appeared to claim Pam.

The playroom was at the rear of the house, a warm, cheery room with paneled walls and brightly slip-covered furniture. In one corner a boy and girl were playing Ping-pong; others were gathered around a card table. Then Dick came toward them from where he had been talking to two older couples standing by the fireplace. "So you finally got here," he teased. "Don't you know you're supposed to be early? You're not living up to your reputation."

Betty flushed as she remembered that first date when she had been waiting for Dick so obviously. But she grinned impudently. "Well, you see it was this way: I ran into a little excitement today. Of course, it was nothing important."

Dick chuckled as he tucked his arm under hers. "Come on, I want you to meet my parents."

Betty would have recognized Dick's father anywhere: that same lean, rangy build, those little crinkles at the corners of his eyes. He shook her hand warmly. Mrs. Ackerman was a beautiful woman, with sculptured white hair that contrasted with her deep fuchsia dress. A pair of cool blue eyes swept Betty's face, eyes as cold as the fingertips she extended. "So this is Betty—Dick's little Mexican friend."

There was a sudden thickness in Betty's throat. In one word . . . in a single, accented, prejudiced word, the wonderful bubble of victory had been shattered. Somehow Betty bobbled through those next minutes of conversation, an introduction to the McMillans, who were the other couple, a discussion of the election. At last, with a feeling of relief, she heard Dick suggesting that they join the others for the dancing.

As soon as they moved away, Mrs. Ackerman turned back to her conversation. A single fragment trailed after them: "Well, you know how Dick is—always taking up some cause . . ." Betty made it through the doorway, two scarlet spots flaming in her cheeks.

"You know, my folks like you." Dick squeezed her arm as they went down the hall. "I could see they liked you right off."

"I liked them too; they're a lovely couple." Betty was surprised that her voice could ring with such false warmth, when inside all she felt was bleak coldness. Dick hadn't even noticed his mother's remark! Could it be . . . could it be that was how he thought of her too, how he'd described her to his family?

In the living room, Betty stepped into Dick's arms. Her

small shoulders were stiff; they danced in silence. Suddenly it was gone, all the easy, laughing banter, the warm comradeship between them. When the music stopped, they changed partners with Roger and Agnes. Roger, with his long, loose-jointed legs, was a clumsy dancer; as they moved off he was already stumbling over Betty's feet. From across Agnes' shoulder, Dick sent her an understanding grin. But Betty turned her head coldly. Even when Dick's puzzled eyes trailed after her, she told herself miserably that she didn't care.

Later, as Betty stood with Roger helping him select a new stack of records, Laurel joined them. Her wide, heavy-lashed eyes were bright with friendliness. "You'll make a marvelous Commissioner, Betty, a lot better than I would have been." Her pretty face twisted into a little grimace. "I guess it's back to the Drama Society for me. That's where I belong. At least I hope I belong . . . I won't know until after the next tryouts."

As Betty looked into those dancing hazel eyes, she was suddenly ashamed of herself for ever having called Laurel a snob. She remembered her own secret vow to throw herself into art work if she lost the election. She wondered if Laurel had made a similar promise. "Of course, you'll get the lead in the class play, Laurel," she burst out impulsively. "Why, everyone knows you're the best actress in the school!"

"Oh, Betty, I love you!" Laurel laughed and spun around to Owen, who had just joined them. "Did you hear that, Owen? Betty thinks I'm a cinch to get the lead in the play. No wonder everyone likes her—she's on our side."

Defeat didn't come as easily to Owen. For him the race had been hard and bitter, but he forced a smile. "After today I'd say she was a pretty good person to have on anyone's side."

By now Roger had mastered the mechanism of the record player. He invited Laurel to dance. That left Betty and Owen alone. "Well, congratulations are in order, I guess." Owen's voice was begrudging. Betty thanked him. An awkward silence lengthened between them.

"There's just one thing I'd like to get straight," Owen blurted suddenly, his handsome face reddening. "That deal about your posters . . . well, I want you to know I didn't have anything to do with it. I may have wanted that office pretty bad—but I'm no louse!"

As Betty looked at his struggling face, she was aware of a sudden warm melting. "I know you didn't, Owen," she told him. "Let's forget it."

Forget it. As Betty danced with a short boy in a checked sport jacket, a tall boy with a crew cut, she knew that was what she should do. She would forget that incident back there in the playroom. It was a wonderful party. Everyone was having a good time. But how could she forget? How could she forget when what should have been the happiest evening of her life had suddenly been ruined?

Shortly after midnight hamburgers were served in the playroom. When Dick motioned that there was an empty seat at his table, Betty ignored him. Taking her sandwich, she joined Agnes and Roger on the stairway in the hall. Finally the party was over. Betty wished there was some way she could slip out without saying good-by to her hosts, but she knew it would be unspeakably rude. As she stood in the doorway, her head was high and her farewell included the three of them. "I had a lovely time. It was very kind of you to let me come *tonight*." The careful accent on the last word would leave no doubt in Mrs. Ackerman's mind, no worry that she expected to return again. Leaving Dick to follow her with another one of those baffled looks, she swept grandly down the steps.

"It was a wonderful party." Agnes stretched lazy arms across her pillow.

"Dreamy," Betty agreed with an enthusiasm she didn't feel.

Mrs. Barnes had warned the two of them not to lie awake all night whispering. The warning wasn't needed. It had been a long and exciting day. A few minutes later, Agnes' voice trailed away in the middle of a sleepy sentence and there was only the sound of her deep, regular breathing.

Betty squirmed on the unfamiliar mattress. Outside, the street light made a silvery pattern through the big oak on the Barnes' front lawn. At home the bedroom was in the back; it was cozily dark. Her mind reviewed the events of the day, and with each retelling that incident in the playroom became more important.

Was she in love with Dick? Working together, being together so constantly, had she been guilty of putting some romantic light on their friendship? It would have been easy with Buz and Pam moony over each other, and even Agnes interested in Roger Eaton. If she had felt that way, Betty knew it was over now. Mrs. Ackerman's cold eyes had left no doubt that Betty Ochoa was not the girl for her son. But that wasn't the important thing. They were all too young, they all had too many years ahead of them to get caught up in something serious this soon—even Buz and Pam.

Her friendship with Dick was what mattered. Surely she wasn't just another cause to him? Then as Betty remembered how Dick had fought for her in this election, their long conversations, their plans, she knew that even to hold such a thought was like a betrayal. Dick wasn't responsible for his mother's feelings. Why, the prejudice she had seen on Mrs. Ackerman's face tonight was the very thing she and Dick were fighting. Suddenly she was ashamed of the way she had acted, ashamed of herself for letting a few ill-chosen words ruin a perfect evening.

With all these thoughts of Dick, it was strange that Pete Flores should suddenly pop into her mind. Pete had said that the two of them were alike. Could it be that Pete was just a little bit right? She was getting pretty touchy about being called Mexican too . . .

10

Revenge

Betty was proud of her new desk in the student government office, even if it was a rather small one tucked away in one of the little cubicles off the back hall. On Monday she called her first meeting of the Activities Commission. There was a moment's misgivings when she first stood up in front of the thirty eager faces of the representatives of the campus clubs; but the meeting proceeded smoothly. All the campus organizations were self-governing, and since this was mid-October their yearly schedules were well under way. There was only one minor dispute, between Beaux Arts and the Latin Club, each of whom wanted the cafeteria on the same evening for a dinner-meeting. It was quickly settled.

It was on Wednesday afternoon, as Betty hurried downstairs from the physics lab for her first meeting of the Student Council, that she felt the greatest thrill. It was here, as representative of the campus organizations, that she would have a voice on the twelve-man major governing body of the school. She had been hoping to have a few minutes with Dick alone. But as she entered the council room, she saw that a half-dozen members were already in their seats and Dick, standing at the head of the table, was busy in consultation with Mr. Dean, the faculty adviser. Betty slid into a vacant seat between Morrie Hallman, Boy's League representative, and Wanda Close, President of the junior class. From across the table a short boy with a freckled, almost childishly round face, shot her a companionable smile. He was carrying a new binder too.

Five minutes later Babs Sutherland and Dave Riordan, the last two members, arrived and Dick called the meeting to order. "Before we proceed with the minutes, I'd like to call your attention to the fact that today, for the first time, we are meeting with a full council table." There was a slight twinkle in Dick's eyes as they traveled down the long table. "Probably you know them already, but I'd like to welcome Betty Ochoa, our new Activities Commissioner, and Bill Sharpless, president of the freshman class."

Betty smiled in acknowledgment. So the freckle-faced boy was the new freshman president—no wonder he didn't look over thirteen. The meeting proceeded in its regular pattern: the reading of the minutes, reports from committee chairmen, old business. Then as Dick launched into the first item of new business, Betty felt a flicker of admiration. He pulled no punches as he brought up the major problem facing the school—that of improving relations with the students of Mexican descent. He pointed out how these students must be encouraged to take part in more campus activities, be made to feel that they had a real place in the student body.

"If you ask me, they don't want a part in school activities," Dave grumbled. "They'd rather be left alone."

Dick rapped sharply, cutting him off. "If you don't mind, I still have the floor. A number of people have spoken to me suggesting some kind of memorial for Gabriel Delgado. Well, I have a suggestion which I think will cover both our problems. As you know the schedule of regular school dances has already been planned for the year. But Gabriel was an alumnus and the alumni are holding their annual Home-coming Dance next month. They have already agreed to make it a Gabriel Delgado Memorial Dance, provided the rest of us will get behind them and make it an all-school affair, with a special invitation to the Mexican-American students and alumni to attend."

There were several enthusiastic nods, Betty's among them. "Something like the Armando Castro Fund," Morrie suggested.

"Armando Castro—who was he?" a voice asked.

Morrie turned his head. "Oh, you must remember—it happened three or four years ago in Los Angeles. This Castro was a Spanish kid, a real right guy. He was killed trying to stop a street fight. The kids at Roosevelt High started a collection; then the junior college, some civic organizations joined in and they gave a big dance. It kept growing; other high schools took it up. Now they give a dance every year and use the money to help a lot of needy kids go on with school."

Dick grinned. "Well, Bellamar is a small town, not Los Angeles. I don't think we could do anything *that* big. But if we could just raise a few hundred dollars we could show the Mexican-Americans we haven't forgotten and are on their side."

"I don't know . . ." Babs put in cautiously. "I don't think we ought to rush into anything." Betty remembered Babs had been one of those who talked loudly about sending the Mexican-Americans to a separate school.

"She's right," Dave agreed. "No use going off half-cocked. We could be asking for trouble. Let the alums take care of it."

Betty glanced around the table. Already the skepticism was reaching the others, the first enthusiasm was dying from their faces. If they let it drop now, they might never bring it up again. A few more weeks and Gabriel's memory would be a little dimmer. Instantly she was on her feet. "Mr. President, I make a motion the Student Council and the entire student body support the alumni in sponsoring a Gabriel Delgado Memorial Dance to be held in November."

"Second," Morrie added the footnote.

"Now just a minute"—Dave lunged to his feet—"I don't like being rushed into things; I haven't had time to say my piece." For the next half-hour the voices rose and fell around the table. They semed equally divided, some for the proposal, some against. Then Babs had the floor again. "I think we're being shoved into this. Oh, the idea of a memorial is okay. But Gabriel wasn't even a student; he graduated two years ago. It doesn't have to be anything as big and important as a dance. I suggest we just take up a collection in the classrooms . . ."

Betty's eyes flew to the clock, a few more minutes and the meeting would end. If Babs kept on talking, if she held the floor, she could stall off the vote.

Then across the way, Bill Sharpless was on his feet.

"Point of order, Mr. President! What Miss Sutherland is suggesting is another motion. May I point out that she can't introduce a new motion when one is already on the floor. I call for a vote."

Betty's eyes sparkled as she flashed Bill a triumphant grin. Maybe he did look like a rosy-cheeked infant, but she knew now why he had been elected. Dick called for the vote. The motion for the Gabriel Delgado Memorial Dance passed by a vote of 7-to-5, just as the hour bell sounded.

Betty gathered her notes and shoved them in the new binder. As the disgruntled losers, still arguing, crowded toward the door, Bab's voice floated back. "Talk about railroading!" Another voice added waspishly. "Well, I warned you. After all, he was her campaign manager, wasn't he? It'll be this way all year, the two of them trying to run the whole show!"

Dick looked down into Betty's suddenly stricken face. "Don't let it bother you. They'll come around." The corners of his mouth quirked into that familiar lopsided grin. "Sometimes, to get things done you have to tromp on a few toes. And if you do, you might as well expect to get tromped on in return. That's democracy—the eloquent minority."

That little imp of good humor returned to Betty's face. "Well, I'm just glad my feet are well calloused already!" Suddenly it had vanished, that momentary disappointment that the council had not been unanimous in this first effort to improve student relations. It was true they had been in the majority. Maybe next time it would not be as easy. But at least the Gabriel Delgado Memorial Dance was a beginning.

Five minutes later Betty waltzed down the broad front steps. It was only when she saw a couple of sophomore girls turning to stare that she broke out of the little tune and slowed to a more sedate walk, appropriate to an upper classman. Spotting a tall figure, shoulders slouched, hands rammed into the pockets of his leather jacket, coming down the path from the Science wing, she stopped where the two walks joined. Any other day she would have hurried ahead to avoid meeting Pete. But today she was too happy and, besides, she remembered she had not thanked him for the part he had played in her election.

"*Hola,*" Pete replied gruffly in Spanish to her greeting. If he was surprised, he quickly recovered with his customary scowl. Betty's footsteps had to quicken to match his long strides. "I've been wanting to talk to you, Pete. I want to thank you."

Pete swung around, the scowl growing blacker. "Thank me for what?"

"For supporting me in the election. Dick said I wouldn't have won it if it hadn't been for you."

Pete dug his fists deeper into his pockets. "You don't need to thank me—thank those *gabacho* friends of yours. I didn't do anything. I didn't even vote."

Betty fought that familiar tide of exasperation. Why did he have to be so impossible, so stubborn? "Well, you put up that poster. And a lot of students voted who never voted before."

"Okay, so you thanked me," Pete admitted grumpily. They had reached the boulevard now and he looked around. "You don't have to walk with me any longer; that is, if you're worried someone might see you."

Betty's face flamed. Honestly, he could be the rudest . . . ! She strangled the scorching anger and forced herself to keep up with him. "Why should I be ashamed to be seen with you? You have a lot of silly ideas."

Pete shrugged, not bothering to reply. But he slowed those long strides in a kind of momentary condescension, so that Betty could abandon the jogging trot that had been necessary to keep up with him. One more block and they would reach the corner of Paloma Road, where she turned off, while Pete continued on to Meridian Avenue. She groped desperately for some topic of conversation to fill the distance.

"I went to my first council meeting this afternoon and guess what we decided," she began eagerly. "The whole school is going to join with the alumni on Home-coming Day for a memorial dance in honor of Gabriel."

"Great!" Pete scoffed. "And I suppose you think that will do him good, now he is dead. You think his *alma* will come back and dance, maybe?"

Betty could feel herself sputtering inside, like the fuse that's been lit on a small firecracker. "Well, at least we'll be doing something! We'll show that he hasn't been forgotten."

"Don't worry, he hasn't been forgotten." Pete's laugh was ugly. "*Los Coyotes* haven't forgotten. When we're finished with *Calle Nueve*, they'll be wishing the cops had put them all in jail."

Betty spun around, her hand reaching for his arm. "Pete, you don't mean that! What good will that do? All this fighting in gangs doesn't solve anything . . . it only makes it hard on the other Mexican-Americans, gives them a bad reputation. You have to leave this to the police."

"The police!" Pete snorted. "We can handle this our own way."

"But Gabriel didn't even belong to *Los Coyotes*," Betty protested.

"They thought he did. That's enough."

"Pete, it's crazy!" Betty shook his arm. "You're smart, Pete, smarter than that. You know if you go into Los Angeles and start a fight with *Calle Nueve*, they'll just come back here again. It'll go on and on. It'll never stop. A lot of fine kids will be hurt, maybe killed."

They had reached Betty's corner now. She thought she saw a flicker of hesitation in his eyes. Then he brushed her hand away roughly. "You don't know anything about it! Just leave me alone," and he plunged away.

Then, almost as abruptly, he swirled and came back. The anger was gone from his dark eyes. When they didn't have that hard, jet look, they could be soft, like dusky velvet. "Look, I lied to you." His voice was almost humble. "I did vote for you and I made all the gang vote too. I'm sorry for what I said about your being ashamed to walk with me."

His black eyebrows drew together and he seized Betty's arm. His fingers were so hard and strong a little pain shot to her elbow. "Only don't walk with me any more. I'm warning you . . . I'm no good for you. Don't even come near me on the street—something could happen, you could be hurt." He was gone, long legs carrying him down the street.

As Betty stared after that cocky, retreating figure, her anger was gone too. In its place was a numbing fear. Something was going to happen, something very bad. She shivered. As she turned down Paloma Road the street didn't look gay and beckoning as before; it was as if a cold gray mist had settled over the friendly houses and bright gardens.

"A rumble," the kids called it at school: whispers, gossip, little groups talking in corners. Some said *Los Coyotes* had challenged *Calle Nueve* to an open battle; others said they were planning a secret raid. But no one had any real facts. Betty noticed that even Mr. Huxley went around with a drawn, preoccupied look on his face those next few days. He had authority over the students at school, but how was he to fight something that was only a rumor, an ugly tension in the air?

Friday afternoon Betty turned down an invitation to join Pam and Agnes at the Black-and-Gold after school.

"Maybe it's love?" Pam goaded hopefully.

"Not love—homework." Betty giggled as she pretended to stagger under her load of books. "An English theme, a Spanish assignment, three experiments in physics."

"See? Three physics assignments," Agnes chirped gleefully. "She's in love with Mr. Mead." They all dissolved in laughter as they imagined Betty falling for the fiftyish, balding, and married physics professor.

"Well, run along then. Don't let us keep you from your secret passion," Pam begrudged.

At the corner of Paloma Road, Betty almost turned back to join those two bright figures already disappearing up the boulevard. Then, remembering how she had been neglecting her schoolwork these last weeks, she tightened her arms around the heavy stack of books and continued resolutely toward home. Friday was Larry's afternoon for Cub Scouts and Mrs. Ochoa's meeting of the Altar Society at the church. Even Gloria apparently had stayed after school on some excuse. It wasn't unusual for Larry and Gloria to be away with their friends; Betty decided it was her mother's absence that made the house seem so lonely. In the kitchen, she poured herself a glass of milk and, arranging some crackers on a plate, carried them into her room.

But working at the small desk, she found it impossible to concentrate. Somewhere in the distance there was the thin wail of a siren. Ruffles, in protest against the disagreeable sound, howled mournfully. She came over to drop her head in Betty's lap, where she looked at her mistress out of the top of sorrowful spaniel eyes.

"All right, all right." Betty closed her book disgustedly. "I might as well take you for a run—you won't give me any peace until I do."

In the sunny back yard Betty sent an old rubber ball careening against the back fence. Ruffles charged after it with a yelp of delight, raced back to drop it at Betty's feet. She bounced the ball off the fence again. It fell in obvious sight in front of a large chrysanthemum plant. But Ruffles, already tired of the game, ran to the back gate where she began sniffing eagerly.

"Silly, it didn't go over the fence. It's right here." Betty stooped to retrieve the ball. Raffles refused to turn her head. The sniffing was more persistent now, accompanied by small whines.

Betty's voice was annoyed. "There's no one in the alley either. The trash man came this morning." To prove the point she flung open the gate.

There was a sudden movement as a tall figure flattened against the redwood fence.

"Pete!" Betty gasped. "What are you doing here?"

"Nothing." Pete's voice was husky, his face tight-lipped and ashen. "I . . . I was just taking a short cut home." Then as he moved away from the fence, he swayed slightly and Betty saw the arm pressed uselessly against his side, the crimson stain spreading down his jeans across the back of his free hand as he tried vainly to staunch the flow of blood with the corner of his jacket.

Before she could let out a horrified cry, there was the scream of a siren on the next block. "Pete, you didn't . . . ?"

"I didn't hurt anyone. . . ." The words came in broken little spurts. "Didn't have a chance . . . three guys from

Calle Nueve jumped me. . . ." The siren was closer now, turning onto the street at the end of the alley.

Almost without thinking, Betty grabbed Pete's arm, jerked him into her yard, and slammed the gate. The two of them clung together, pressed against the fence, as the car slowed at the entrance to the alley. Then it moved on again, slowly up the street.

11

Doctor Jim

Betty let out her breath in a small escaping sigh as the siren faded into the distance. She felt Pete's shoulders relax, though she could still feel the hammering of his heart through the heavy jacket. Releasing her, he stepped back and sank onto the wooden bench of the picnic table at the edge of the lawn.

Across Betty's white blouse was a pink stain where they had stood pressed together. The sight of the blood brought her back to reality. "Your arm, Pete—we have to do something."

Ordinarily Betty was uncomfortable at the sight of blood, but she fought down the squeamish feeling in her stomach. It was an ugly wound, extending halfway from his wrist to his elbow. Her mind flew frantically back to some half-forgotten first-aid lesson. If the blood came in spurts, the artery was severed. This wasn't coming in spurts, but it was a steady flow and there was too much of it.

"Come into the house. I'll get a bandage," Betty ordered.

Pete hesitated, eyes wary. For a moment Betty thought that now the siren was gone he was going to dart back to the alley. She tossed her dark curls. "It's all right. Nobody is home."

On the back porch Betty found some gauze on the emergency shelf above the washing machine. When Pete released the pressure of his fingers, the blood came brighter, but a few swift, tight turns of the bandage and it slowed again. Betty wrapped the length of the cut, not satisfied until she had used the entire roll of gauze, finishing it off with another tight knot. It was not a professional job, but it would do.

"Thanks!" Some of the color had returned to Pete's face; he fumbled awkwardly for a cigarette. "Well, guess I'd better be going." As he bent to pick up his jacket, Betty let out a startled cry. Just the slight movement and his arm was bleeding again, the red stain immediately coming through the thick layers of bandage.

"Pete, you can't go anywhere! Your arm—it needs stitches. I'm going to call Dr. Evans."

"No you don't!" Pete seized her wrist. "It's all right. I tell you, I'm fine now . . . I don't need any doctor." But that spreading crimson, the way he staggered slightly, made a lie of the words.

"Pete!" Betty's voice was frightened. The sudden thought popped into her mind that maybe he couldn't afford a doctor. Then she remembered that horrible day last summer when Larry had fallen out of the apricot tree and broken his arm. Her mother had been unable to reach Dr. Evans; instead they had rushed Larry to a small emergency clinic down on Meridian Avenue. "Pete, you're going to see a doctor. I'll take you to the clinic. If you don't get that arm taken care of it may be crippled; you'll never use it again."

Betty didn't know if it was that last threat, but suddenly Pete's resistance seemed to crumble. He followed her to the garage. Luckily this was the day Mr. Ochoa rode with one of the other men in his car pool, and since Mrs. Ochoa didn't know how to drive, the blue sedan was in its usual place. Pete beside her, Betty backed the car out of the garage.

They turned onto Meridian Avenue, passed the stone and stucco columns of St. Gregory's church, and midway in the next block Betty braked to the curb. The building was little different from the small stores on either side, except that the front windows were curtained with tan monk's cloth and above the door was a sign: *Meridian Avenue Clinic Drs. Oberon and Sanchez.*" Directly above was another sign in red neon tubing: "*Emergency Hospital—24 Hours.*"

By now Pete was slumped forward, head in his hands. Maybe he was sick . . . maybe he had lost too much blood. Scrambling out of the car, Betty raced across the sidewalk and threw open the door. "Miss . . . Miss . . . !" she called.

There was no crisp, starched uniform behind the reception desk; the waiting room appeared deserted. Then a pair of broad shoulders in a rumpled tunic straightened from where they had been half hidden by the files. "I'm afraid Miss Vernon isn't here now. I'm Dr. Sanchez. Will I do?"

Betty colored. He didn't look old enough to be a doctor,

really—that is, not middle-aged and professional-looking like Dr. Evans. He couldn't have been over thirty, short, stocky, with close-cropped black hair and a face that was still boyish in spite of the thin mustache. But there was something about his snapping, dark eyes that inspired confidence.

"I have a friend outside—he's badly hurt." Betty's voice cracked a little. She looked frantically over her shoulder, worried that Pete might try to slip away. "I'm not sure he'll come in . . ."

Then before the doctor could reply, Pete, who had got out of the car, now shoved into the doorway, brows drawn into a belligerent scowl. "What she's trying to say, doc, . . . I got carved in a fight. So if you have any idea of calling the cops on me, let's skip it. I'll just be getting along . . ."

If Betty had expected Dr. Sanchez to be shocked by Pete's bluntness, she was mistaken. Instead, he laughed. "Why should I call the police? If you *gatos* didn't get yourselves knifed up once in a while, I wouldn't have much business." A second later he was leading Pete through the door at the back of the waiting room. Not knowing what else to do, Betty followed.

She was sure she had never seen anyone work so fast. Dr. Sanchez already had Pete sitting on the white-topped examining table. Scissors snipped through the knots of the bandage and he was unwinding the spirals. Embarrassed, Pete glowered in Betty's direction. But before she could retreat, the doctor, tossing the crumpled bandage into a container, called her back. "Hey you, stay here. My nurse won't be back for an hour and I may need some help."

As Betty stepped back into the room, Dr. Sanchez grinned at the two of them. "You can call me Dr. Jim. And you might as well tell me your names because we're going to be here for quite a while. This thing is going to take a dozen stitches."

While Dr. Jim cleaned the wound, calling from time to time for Betty to hand him medicine or cotton from a small side table, he kept up a running flow of talk. "Now it's clean. I'll just give you a little something to deaden the pain while I put in the sutures."

Pete jerked back. "You aren't giving me anything. I can stand it!" he bristled.

"I know *you* can," Dr. Jim snapped back. "But *I* can't. Wiggle just a little and I'll make a mess of a job. It's only a local. That is, unless you're afraid of a little needle?" Before Pete could protest, strong brown fingers had pinioned his arm and the pain-killing injection was going under the skin. Looking sheepish, Pete relaxed.

"Must have been quite a beef?" Dr. Jim inquired as he prepared to make the first suture.

Pete shrugged. "Nothing much. Three guys from *Calle Nueve* jumped me on the way home from school."

"Going to let them get away with it?"

"Of course not!" Pete flared. "We'll show 'em."

Dr. Jim motioned to Betty to hand him more antiseptic. "You think you have a pretty good 'gang' huh?"

"You bet we have!" Pete's face flushed angrily. "Say, what's it to you anyhow? What're you getting so nosey for?"

Instead of looking annoyed, Dr. Jim shrugged. "It's nothing to me. Just making conversation. I used to belong to the 'Avenues.' Of course, that was a long time ago. We were pretty tough."

It was Betty's turn to be shocked. Even she knew that the "Avenues" was a notorious Los Angeles gang. But Pete had straightened, eyes suddenly interested. "You mean you always lived around here?"

"Not in Bellamar, but Los Angeles, if that's what you mean. Born in Los Angeles, went to school there, got my medical degree there, interned at General Hospital . . ." Dr. Jim's deft fingers completed another stitch. "I remember one time we had a rumble going with 'White Fence,' or was it 'Alpine'? Anyhow it was a real beef, or at least we thought it was going to be. We knew they had a couple of zip guns, but we had plenty of bicycle chains, tire irons, the works. We planned to meet outside the *barrio* in this little park out in the Valley where we could really mix it. Well, we got out there about ten o'clock at night, pitch-black, six carloads of us. We started piling out of the cars when suddenly everywhere, lights are going on. Must have been half the Valley police force, just sitting there in the dark waiting for us . . . never did find out who tipped them off." He laughed. "Guess it was a good thing though. Otherwise I might not be here today, stitching you up."

Pete was relaxed now and smiling. "I've heard about the Avenues. They're okay."

Dr. Jim had finished the last suture and was putting on the bandage. "Some afternoon you and the fellows ought to come down to the Almansor Street Center. We just started last year, but we have a pretty sharp bunch of boys. We still have to use the grammar school grounds for our diamond, but we've fixed up that old warehouse next door for a clubhouse."

As quickly as Pete's interest had flared, it vanished. His eyes narrowed suspiciously. "I thought there was some hitch—trying to soften me up with all this buddy talk. Look, don't give me any preaching. I'm not interested in joining any good-deeds club. I don't want anything to do with it!"

Angered at Pete's rudeness, Betty quickly looked at the

doctor, but Dr. Jim just chuckled. "Suit yourself. You're probably right, anyhow. Anyone who can't handle himself in a knife fight any better than you can wouldn't stand much of a chance with my boys." He gave the bandage a final pat. "There . . . I'll want to see that again in about three days. Only be sure you come here instead of the Center. I wouldn't want you to get your other arm injured . . . our boys know judo."

Pete's face was purple. "What d'ya mean saying I can't fight? I can take care of myself! I don't need any judo, any doctor. . . ." Without thanking the doctor or Betty for their help, he slid from the table and snatched his leather jacket from a chair. Throwing it over his shoulder, so that even the white coyote seemed to snarl at them, he slammed out of the office without another word.

Betty was so embarrassed that she didn't know what to say. Somehow she mumbled her thanks to Dr. Jim and turned to escape too. But he called her back and motioned to a chair by his desk. "Just a minute. I'd like to talk to you."

Gingerly Betty eased herself onto the chair. Feeling the candid scrutiny of those dark eyes, she shifted uncomfortably. Probably he wanted to be paid. She had only a dollar in her purse.

"Guess I'm just a curious guy or something. So if you think I'm getting too 'nosey,' as Pete calls it, you tell me." Dr. Jim leaned forward, a smile tugging at the corners of his mouth. "But just what connection does a girl like you have with Pete Flores? You can't be his *wisa*?"

"*Wisa?*" Betty's nose wrinkled and her eyes shot little sparks. "How I hate that word—all that *pachuco* talk! Of course I'm not Pete's girl. This afternoon I was home studying, when all of a sudden Ruffles—that's our dog—

started sniffing at the gate. There was Pete in the alley, so. . . ." Then with that friendly understanding shining in Dr. Jim's eyes and knowing how confused her story must sound, she told him everything—about the encounter at school, the night Mrs. Flores came to the house, Pete's help in her election.

When she had finished, Dr. Jim nodded. "You know, Betty, a girl like you could help Pete a lot. In fact, I suspect you have helped him already."

Just remembering Pete's rudeness, the way he had rushed into the street without thanking either of them, brought an angry knot to Betty's throat. "I'm not sure I want to help him!" she exploded. "Only every time I turn around—there he is! Oh, I know he's probably smart enough underneath, and he is good-looking, but well . . . well, he's just so *awful*!"

Dr. Jim laughed, an immense laugh that seemed to sweep up right from his toes. It reminded Betty of Uncle Jaime and suddenly she was laughing too. "I agree with you, Pete is pretty awful," Dr. Jim was still chuckling. "But I agree with you also that he's an intelligent boy. Maybe when we get him down to the Almansor Street Center we can rub off some of those rough spots."

Betty's laughter trickled away. Dr. Jim was so nice; he'd tried to be so helpful. It made her feel sorry to disillusion him. "I know Pete, Dr. Jim," she told him. "He won't come to the Center. I can tell you right now, you won't ever interest him in a group like that."

Dr. Jim's chair scraped along the floor as he stood up. "I wouldn't be too sure about that, Betty," he said. "I wouldn't be too sure at all."

12

Big Problems

Somehow those weeks passed quickly, days pyramiding one upon another with only the week ends bringing brief pinnacles of respite until another ambitious Monday started the same dizzy climb. Weekly council meetings, football games, homework, selling tickets for the Delgado Memorial Dance—sometimes Betty had the feeling that time was swirling by so quickly she couldn't catch her breath. There hadn't been time to think about Pete Flores, except for a brief nod if she happened to pass him in the halls, her small feet going at the sharp ra-ta-tap that had become her trade-mark these last days. There hadn't been time to think about *Los Coyotes* either, except to be thankful that the police had arrested the two boys responsible for Gabriel's death and a closer survelliance of the Meridian area had temporarily quieted the gang activities.

One Friday noon, juggling tray, art portfolio, and the familiar red binder, Betty joined Pam and Agnes at a table in the cafeteria, where they always ate on Fridays. For Pam and Agnes it was the only day they condescended to sacrifice the intimacy of their beloved threesome and join their classmates. For Betty it was something more. Unlike some Catholics, she had a real passion for sea food. On Fridays the cafeteria featured a thick clam chowder that was beyond description.

"How can you eat that same stuff week after week?" Pam sniffed disdainfully as she poked at a delicate lettuce and egg salad. Pam had blossomed these last weeks since she and Buz were openly going steady, though young love had done nothing for her appetite.

"You don't eat soup. You spoon it," Agnes corrected.

"You eat this . . . it's that thick!" Betty looked up for the briefest moment. "Besides, I need the nourishment to keep up the dizzy pace of existence—to stave off the ravages of time." She liked the succulent thickness of the clichés.

"Who's this, who's battling the ravages of time?" a jovial voice interrupted as Dick leaned over the table.

"Betty"—Agnes bobbed her head in her friend's direction—"she's aging prematurely. We were just counting her gray hairs."

Dick laughed. "Well, I wouldn't count on getting paid for each one I find. And speaking about counting, how are the ticket sales?"

"Don't look at me," Pam grimaced. "I couldn't sell a hand-warmer to an Eskimo."

"I've sold two books . . . twenty tickets," Agnes replied.

"Good girl," Dick beamed. "I just got rid of my fourth book."

"You would!" Betty wrinkled her nose. "I still have five left in my fourth book. It's so late now, I'll probably have to eat them."

"They're not very filling and it'll cost you five dollars." His face was suddenly serious. "About those other tickets, Betty—you've taken care of them, haven't you?"

The giggle died on Betty's lips; her hand moved to the little clutch purse on the papers beside her. "Not yet, Dick, but I'll deliver them this afternoon, I promise."

As he moved on to another table, Agnes and Pam went back to their bantering conversation. But not Betty; her eyes strayed again to the small purse. Because of all the members of the Student Council she was the closest to the Delgado family, she had been asked to present Carla with two complimentary tickets to the dance. She was ashamed to admit how she had been dreading the task. Since the funeral, except for a hasty "hello" as she passed the attendance office, she hadn't talked with Carla since Gabriel's death. What did one say? How did one find the right words? Sometimes walking home from school she passed the Delgado house. Mrs. Delgado in her black dress and shawl sat on the front porch rocking quietly in a big chair, her face so unbelievably sad that a little knife of agony pierced Betty's heart.

It was three-thirty when Betty approached the attendance office timidly. Carla glanced up from the desk behind the counter. "Why, hello, Betty." She smiled. "What are you doing here . . . been cutting classes again?"

Betty knew she was teasing. Some of her fears melted before that merry, normal smile. "Not exactly. I stopped by because I wanted—I mean the Student Council and I wanted . . ." She was making a miserable botch of it. "Here, these are tickets for the dance. We know how you feel—probably you won't want to come. But we'd be honored if you did and we want you to have the tickets anyhow."

It was no more than a whisper, that little flicker of pain in Carla's eyes, then she accepted the tickets with a smile. "Thank you, Betty. I am honored too. Gabriel would be very happy. It really is too soon to go to a dance—but in this case I think we might make an exception. Only I want to help. Couldn't I buy a couple of tickets too?"

"Could you? Oh, Carla, you've saved my life!" With eager fingers Betty was already opening her stub book. Leaving the office five minutes later, she was more than ever ashamed of herself for having dreaded the interview. That was the trouble, she told herself severely, she always took things so seriously, imagining what people were going to say without even giving them a chance.

Emboldened by the encounter with Carla, Betty accosted Carmen Ortiz and her friend, Jenny Lopez, in the hall. They weren't quite so easy to convince; but five minutes later Betty had sold each of them a ticket too. That left only one in her book. She saw Pete Flores coming across the grass from the gym field. In her enthusiasm Betty forgot all about that angry scene at the clinic. "Hey, Pete! Pete, wait!" she called.

The tall boy spun around. His face had a strangely jumbled look: eyes warm with welcome but lips remaining sullen and compressed, too proud to reveal his true feelings. Betty refused to be daunted, even though she couldn't resist one peppery little dig. "What's wrong—too proud to be seen with me?"

It was Pete's turn to redden. For a moment Betty was afraid she had gone too far; he was so touchy. Then his mouth broadened in a dazzling grin. "Of course I'm too proud . . . who wants to be seen with a little *pocha* like you?"

Betty flinched at the slang expression. *Pocha* was the word for a California-born Mexican with fair skin. But Pete had not said the word in anger; for a moment there was some of that same crinkly, teasing look around his eyes that she saw so often in Dick's. Once again Betty couldn't help noticing how handsome Pete was. It was more than just dark curly hair and regular features. There was something about the way he walked, lithe, sure-footed, the masculine swagger of his shoulders, a feeling of hidden strength. She couldn't help thinking that if she was in real physical danger, she would like to have Pete around.

To break the silence that somehow always had a way of lengthening between them, she jumped to her reason for calling him. "Are you going to the dance tomorrow night?" Her hand squeezed the small purse with the one ticket left. "If you haven't bought your ticket yet, I'd like to sell it to you."

Pete shrugged. "I don't dance."

"Don't give me that!" Betty teased. "You're a good dancer. I saw you at the church *jamaica* last summer. You know this is a pretty special dance. You liked Gabriel. I just sold tickets to Carmen and Jenny."

Pete's shoulders slouched forward. "I don't have a girl."

Betty knew that wasn't true. There were plenty of girls on Meridian Avenue who would jump at a chance to go anywhere with Pete.

Her eyes sparkled. "You dance. You *do* have a girl. You'll have to give me a better reason than that."

Once again he flashed that wide grin. "You never give up, do you?"

It was fun finding Pete so pleasant and friendly. "You just said it yourself," she told him tartly. "Since I never give up, you have to give in. You have to buy that ticket now."

For a moment they walked in silence. Then Pete stopped so abruptly that his arm caught hers, spinning her around with him. "All right, I will buy a ticket," he said. "But I was telling the truth when I said I didn't have a girl. I'll buy a ticket and go to the dance—if you'll go with me."

Caught unaware, Betty struggled to catch her breath. Go to a dance with Pete—Pete Flores, the leader of the notorious *Los Coyotes*? For a moment she could imagine the absolutely horrified expression on everyone's face . . . Pam, Agnes, Dick . . . even her own parents. Of course, Pete was only teasing. Then as she met those dark eyes holding hers so intently, she knew that wasn't true. Pete wasn't teasing. He was serious.

"Pete, I'm terribly sorry but I . . ." Even as the words left her lips, Betty realized that she had waited too long. "I already have a date—I mean I've made arrangements." How could she explain when it wasn't exactly a date? Just Sybil, Dodie, Agnes, Roger, Tom, all the gang, going together the way they always had since their freshman days.

But Pete had caught that moment of hesitation. The teasing laughter, the flashing grin were gone. The eyes that could be like warm velvet became jet stones again. "You wouldn't be caught dead with me," Pete snapped. "That's what you're really trying to say, isn't it? That Pete—that *pachuco*!"

"Pete, that isn't true! I have another date already. Pete, we're still friends," Betty pleaded.

But he ignored the small hand extended to him. "You've made it. You've crossed the tracks. You're on the other side now. Well, why don't you stay where you belong?" he said savagely, a bleak, stricken look in his eyes. "Stay on your own side. Stop coming around me and messing up my life!"

There was a choking lump in Betty's throat, her eyes stung childishly.

"Hi, kids, going my way?" The ringing voice saved her as a small coupe slid to the curb. It took a moment to recognize Dr. Jim's square face and trim mustache through a blurry haze. He reached to open the door. "Hop in . . . I'll give you both a lift."

"Don't bother about me." Pete's voice was cutting. "I'd rather walk—alone!"

Betty watched him swing off down the street, the white coyote on his jacket jeering back at her. Again she felt that choking misery. Dr. Jim's voice steadied her. "Well, one customer deserted me, but I can still drive you home, can't I?" Nodding automatically, Betty got into the car.

"Beautiful day, really ought to make you walk—good for the circulation," Dr. Jim commented as he put the car in gear. Betty stared out the window. In spite of her best efforts one enormous tear spilled down her cheek.

Suddenly her head snapped around. They had already passed Paloma Road. "My street—it's back there!"

If Dr. Jim saw the tear she brushed away so hurriedly on the pretense of patting her hair, he gave no sign. He kept his eyes on the road. "You aren't in any rush, are you? I still have a half-hour before I go on duty at the clinic. Never heard of a girl your age turning down an invitation for a free Coke."

They were headed in the opposite direction from the Black-and-Gold. On Meridian Avenue, Dr. Jim stopped in front of El Tipo Café. By now most of the after-school crowd had gone; there were only a few girls sitting at the counter. Dr. Jim steered Betty to a small booth at the rear. The arrival of a cherry Coke washed down part of the lump in her throat. Then as her straw explored the bottom of the glass, she looked up to see Dr. Jim studying her.

"It looked to me like you and Pete were having quite an argument," he said. "Have a problem, Betty? Sometimes it helps to talk it out—and I'm a good listener."

Once again Betty had that feeling of Dr. Jim's sincerity. He wasn't just being polite; he was really interested. Before she realized it, she was telling him about the encounter, Pete's invitation to the dance, and his vicious anger when she refused. Now she was all upset, her whole beautiful week end was ruined.

When she had finished, Dr. Jim nodded sympathetically. He stirred his coffee. "Did you ever have this come up before, Betty? I mean, have you ever had other boys ask you for a date when you already had one?"

"Of course." Betty was puzzled. "It's happened a few times before. I just explained that I was sorry but I had made other arrangements."

Dr. Jim's eyes narrowed shrewdly. "Naturally. It's one of those things that happen all the time. It isn't the girl's fault. It isn't the boy's fault—except possibly that he should have asked the girl a little earlier. Tell me, these other times when you turned down a boy, did you get so upset about it?"

"Not at all. Oh sure, I felt sorry. But then they didn't act like Pete, they . . ." Betty's voice trailed away under that searching gaze. Suddenly she knew what Dr. Jim was trying to tell her, what he was trying to make her see for herself. What had happened this afternoon was unfortunate, but it was one of those things that were bound to happen now and then. Why, then, should a simple thing like turning down a date with Pete upset her so terribly? Unless their relationship wasn't quite as casual as she pretended—unless he really meant something to her.

Betty felt the blush streaking up her throat, spreading across her cheeks. But she wasn't interested in Pete Flores! She couldn't be!"

As though sensing her embarrassment, Dr. Jim grinned and reached for his wallet, changing the subject. "That last ticket of yours—how about selling it to me? You know, I'm not such an old fogey but what I still go to a dance now and then. Several of my friends are Bellamar alumni and I think they are going."

Sunny smile restored, Betty opened her purse and tore the last ticket from the book. Dr. Jim placed in carefully in his wallet. "Don't worry about Pete," he told her. "I promise he'll recover. I'll have a little talk with him the next time he comes down to the Almansor Street Center."

"The Almansor Street Center?" Betty gasped. "You mean Pete really came?"

"Sure he came. I told you he would."

"No! Not Pete . . . but why?"

"*Machismo*," Dr. Jim explained with a laugh.

Bewildered, Betty mouthed the half-familiar Spanish word. "I still don't understand."

Dr. Jim's smile broadened. "I wouldn't expect you to; you're a woman. It's something Pete and the others in *Los Coyotes* feel, something every boy and man feels, something I feel too. Only maybe we Spanish-speaking people are a little more honest; at least we have a word for it. There isn't a good English translation, except something like 'he-man.' It's pride, courage, the need to prove to the world that you are a real man, that you aren't afraid of anything. You know, we Mexicans are a proud people. To a boy like Pete who has so little, so few advantages, sometimes all that is left to him is that pride. When I accused Pete of being a poor fighter, I hurt his pride. He had to come to the Center, if for no other reason than to show me up."

Dr. Jim motioned to Ernestina to bring their check. "I only hope now that I can keep him coming. He's quite a baseball player—we could use him on our team this year."

Betty stared down at her glass. She knew that in just a few brief words Dr. Jim had given her an understanding of Pete that she had never had before. "*Machismo,*" she repeated softly. "That's what is behind a lot of the gangs and the street fighting too, isn't it?"

"Partly," Dr. Jim agreed. "Some of the boys are poor like Pete. The United States, in spite of being the wonderful country it is, hasn't quite lived up to their dreams. Some are better off than they ever were back in Mexico. But either way, Bellamar is full of people who are prejudiced. The boys never have the feeling of really belonging. They are torn between the old ways of the parents, whom they have rejected, and the new ways of the Americans, who have rejected them. The gang is their one way for expression, one way they can keep their identity. No healthy, red-blooded Mexican man is ever going to let himself become a nonentity."

"Especially not Pete Flores!" Betty added with a little trill of laughter. It was surprising how, after this short talk with Dr. Jim, the day had brightened again.

Outside, she refused to let him drive her home. The walk would do her good; she had some things she wanted to think about.

13

We Won't Forget

"Should I wear the red scarf—or does the blue look better?" Betty stood in front of the dresser mirror holding a filmy scrap of chiffon against the collar of her white jersey blouse.

"Yes, dear." Mrs. Ochoa paused in the doorway. "It looks very nice."

"Oh, Mother!" Betty's voice was petulant. "What kind of answer is that—yes, dear? Which one?"

Resignedly Mrs. Ochoa rested a corner of the vacuum cleaner she was carrying. "Well, I think perhaps the red . . ."

"Mother!" Betty repeated. "I've already put on the blue!"

"Red. Blue. What difference does it make?" Mrs. Ochoa laughed. "You'd think today was some kind of holiday."

Red scarf freshly knotted at her throat, Betty twirled her mother in a joyous hug. "But, Mamma, it is a holiday! Next to graduation it's the most important day of the year." Then snatching her brown coat from the bed, she was racing down the hall and the front door slammed behind her.

It seemed strange to be walking to school at ten o'clock on a Saturday morning. As a freshman, Betty had felt no enthusiasm for Home-coming. But now that she was a senior it was different. There would be the familiar faces of former classmates among the returning alumni. This morning she would act as a guide showing the older alumni around the campus. At noon there would be a luncheon in the cafeteria, in the afternoon the final game of the football season. Betty knew she would miss most of the game, for she would be busy helping decorate the gym for the dance that night. But if she was lucky, she might see the final quarter.

As Betty neared the school, she saw a long ribbon of parked cars already lining the curb. She was hoping to find Dick. She wanted to tell him about her conversation with Dr. Jim.

Dick wasn't alone. Standing in the doorway to the attendance office, he was talking to Laurel. Their blond heads were close together and they were laughing. As Betty watched, Laurel's pretty face tilted provocatively, her hand brushed Dick's shoulder in a possessive gesture. "I'll pick you up at eight," he said. "We don't want to miss the most important dance of the year."

Dick was taking Laurel to the dance! A raw, burning sensation in her throat, Betty spun around and pretended to study the bulletin board. Then certain that neither had seen her, she hurried back the way she had come, around the corner and down the stairs toward her locker on the lower floor.

What was wrong with her? Just because Dick was taking Laurel to the dance—after all, they'd practically gone steady last year. She knew she was being silly. But even the mental scolding wasn't enough to ease that lonely, miserable feeling.

As she reached the bottom of the stairs, there was the sound of bounding footsteps behind her. "Hey! What do you mean giving an old friend the brush-off?" Dick spun her around to face him. "I thought I saw you at the bulletin board, then I turned around and you had disappeared."

Betty could feel her face growing pink, but she forced a pert retort. "I'm magic."

"I'll say you are." Dick whistled. "A regular Houdini, pulling a vanishing act just when I wanted to talk to you. You're going to the dance tonight, aren't you?"

"Natch . . . how else do you suppose I got rid of those forty tickets?" Betty was surprised that her voice could be so laughing and casual. They were at her locker now. She put the brown coat away and took out the small red badge that marked her as a student guide. When she had trouble with the fastener, Dick stepped forward to pin it to her collar. His gray eyes were very close to hers.

"Well, I just wanted to be sure that you saved a couple of dances for me. I'm taking Laurel; we're double-dating with Babs and Dave. But none of this going-steady business, dancing with one partner all evening, for me. Now you promise, we'll trade a couple dances?"

Betty was aware of a sudden warmth dissolving the horrible tightness in her throat. It was just a casual date. Dick and Laurel weren't going steady again after all. It was surprising what a difference it made. As they started back up the stairs, her feet had sprouted feathers. "Someone is going to be at the dance tonight whom I'd like you to meet," she told Dick.

"Great," he beamed. "I hope she's a good dancer."

"Silly, it isn't a *she*—it's a *he*. His name is Dr. Sanchez. He's pretty young for a doctor though, and he works down at the Meridian Clinic. I met him through Pete Flores. He's helped Pete a lot. Dick, I think maybe Dr. Sanchez could help us too."

They had reached the main floor now, and before Betty could continue, a couple in their mid-thirties, with yellow alumni tags on their coats, had come through the door. "Could you tell us if a Mr. Mead still teaches physics here?" the woman asked.

"Tell you about it later . . ." Betty flung back over her shoulder as she started down the hall with the couple on her first official duty of the day

The Gabriel Delgado Memorial Dance was a success; Betty sensed it the moment she came through the door that night. It was true the decorations were hardly as novel as the ones Gabriel had suggested for the first dance of the year; but Betty had to admit that the gymnasium, with the rainbow-hued streamers of crepe paper and a floating cloud of balloons over the center of the floor, was attractive enough for the most discriminating. But best of all was the number of people still streaming through the wide doorway an hour after the dance had started. Many were alumni, older and with faces that were unfamiliar; but there was a good representation from the school too. There was even a sizable crowd from Meridian Avenue. Some of them really could dance. Once Betty saw Carmen dancing with Benny Ruiz, feet flashing, dark hair tossing, her usual sullen expression lost in the pure rapture of the music. In fact, the two of them were so good that a little circle of dance floor cleared around them until they became aware of their audience and dropped back into the crowd in red-faced embarrassment.

Betty danced with Barney Foster, brother of Sybil and Dodie and a lanky junior-college freshman. She supposed he was her official date since he had come up to the door for her, though there was little individual pairing in their crowd. Later she danced with Tom Evans and Roger Eaton. Only Pam and Buz, true to the tradition of "going steady," danced in rapt self-absorption, never changing partners.

Betty decided that that would be pretty dull, except for moments like the one when the music ended abruptly and there she was with Roger, no other partner in sight. Everyone around them seemed to be in the "steady" category, and Roger was much too polite to abandon her, even if it meant being stuck with her all night. Betty squirmed out of his arm. "Golly, Rog, I see someone I have to speak to. Thanks for the dance."

She wished Roger hadn't looked quite so relieved as he hurried across the floor to where Agnes was standing. Could it be that they, too, would soon join the "steady" ranks? The thought gave Betty a lonely little jab. Then, finding herself smothered in the press of the crowd and not a familiar face in sight, she felt even more lost. Already the music was starting. What did she do now? Retreat gracefully to the powder room or stand along the wall like a sore thumb?

"Hey, there. Hey, shortie!"

Betty didn't particularly care for the nickname, but with

her bare five-foot height it was too appropriate to ignore. A moment later Dick was taking her arm. "Whew! Thought I'd never find you in this beehive. No wonder I lost you at that other dance—you need a pair of stilts in a crowd like this."

"Oh, I manage to get around down here. It's my X-ray eyes," Betty quipped. She gazed up at the top of Dick's head, more than a foot above hers. "At least I never suffer from altitude sickness."

"Ouch." He winced. "Guess that'll teach me not to insult you little guys." Then the banter was gone, more serious talk crowding between them. Though it was hard to be heard above the noise of the band, Dick made the effort. "Tell me more about this Dr. Sanchez. What's the pitch? And how does Pete Flores come into it?"

Betty felt herself stiffening. For a moment she regretted letting Pete's name slip out this morning. "Well, I guess you know Pete got into another fight with *Calle Nueve*. He was hurt and he happened to be passing our house, so I took him to the clinic."

She glanced up at Dick's face to see if he was shocked at her association with the most notorious boy in school. She couldn't blame him. Pam would be . . . Agnes too. But Dick's eyes were unblinking as they met hers. "So that's how you met this Dr. Sanchez. And you think he's pretty nice."

Betty relaxed. " 'Pretty nice' doesn't do him justice, Dick. He's more than that. He understands boys like Pete and the others in *Los Coyotes*. He's been through it all himself; he knows what makes them act the way they do."

Suddenly catching sight of a familiar face in a group of adults along the wall, Betty stopped so abruptly that Dick stumbled over her feet. "There he is now. I'll introduce you."

When Dr. Jim swung around, Betty was surprised to see that his companion was Carla Delgado. "Dr. Jim, I'd like you to meet our student body president, Dick Ackerman," she made the introduction.

Dick stepped forward, hand outstretched. "Glad to meet you, sir. Betty says she thinks you could help us." Seconds later the two of them were completely absorbed in their conversation. Carla nudged Betty. "Come on, I think we might as well go powder our noses."

The locker room of the girl's gym was ablaze with lights. Inside, some twenty girls in gay party frocks were freshening their make-up or chattering in little groups. Babs and Laurel, standing nearest the door, were sharing a Coke from the machine. "I ought to be mad at you, running off with my date so I have to hide my injured pride down here in the dungeon," Laurel told Betty.

She was wearing a dress of soft rose-colored silk with a scoop neckline that set off her golden beauty and the creamy perfection of her throat and arms. Something about the subdued tint made Betty's red velveteen seem garish and overdone in contrast. But she tried to ignore a twinge of jealousy. "You needn't worry," she laughed. "I've been deserted too. He's talking shop—school that is, with Carla's date."

Laurel tossed her curls and her tinkling laugh filled the room. "That guy! Honest, if the whole world took Bellamar High as seriously as he does, none of us would have any dates." Hooking her arm through Babs', she started for the door. Then stopping to put the empty bottle in the rack, she turned back. "By the way, I'm having a little party at my house next Friday. Pam and Agnes are coming. I'd like to have you come too, Betty."

When the girls had gone, Betty stared at her reflection in the mirror. There were glowing spots of excitement in her cheeks that matched the vivid red of her lipstick. She wanted to pinch herself to make sure this was real. An invitation to Laurel's house! She had been accepted by the Northridge crowd. That invitation to Dick's hadn't been merely a courtesy gesture. After all these years she finally had been accepted by the most exclusive crowd at school! Such a joyous feeling welled up inside her that it was all she could do to keep her feet from pirouetting to the strains of dance music drifting faintly from outside.

Back at the gymnasium, someone asked Carla to dance. Once again Betty was trapped in the crowd. Dick was nowhere in sight. But before that lost feeling could come sweeping back, someone touched her arm. "I think it's about time you danced with me—at least I assume that's part of the bargain, after selling me a ticket," Dr. Jim said with a wide grin.

Betty stepped into his arms. He wasn't a particularly good dancer. Or maybe he didn't seem like a good dancer because he didn't try any of the fancy steps she loved so well, Betty decided. But it was pleasant dancing with someone you could talk to without getting a crick in your neck.

"I like your boy friend Dick," Dr. Jim told her.

Betty flushed. "Oh, he isn't my boy friend. I mean we're just good . . . good *friendly* friends."

Dr. Jim chuckled at the description. "I didn't know that was possible nowadays. Speaking of friends, I had a talk with Pete."

Betty's head flew up. "Is he still angry?"

"I don't think he was really ever angry, at least not at

you," Dr. Jim explained. "I think Pete was angry at himself—angry because he didn't know enough to ask a girl to a dance ahead of time, because he didn't know the right way to ask for a date." He hesitated a moment before continuing. "Pete has a lot of good qualities, Betty. He thinks a great deal of you. But unless you're willing to accept Pete just as he is, meet his friendship all the way, I'd be careful about seeing too much of him. Pete would only be hurt and you could have an embarrassing repetition of what happened before."

"You mean he might ask me for another date? But I couldn't go out with someone like Pete Flores!" Betty gasped. Then, her face reddening before Dr. Jim's level stare, she realized how prejudiced and snobbish that must have sounded. "I mean couldn't we just be friends, without dates or anything like that?"

"Could you explain that to Pete?" Dr. Jim probed gently. Then with his usual adroitness at changing the conversation when it had become too embarrassing, he was steering her toward the edge of the dance floor. "Come over here, Betty. I'd like to have you meet some friends of mine. We all belong to a Spanish-speaking club. We call ourselves '*Los Hildagos.*' "

A moment later they had joined the group of young adults Betty had noticed earlier in the evening. Except for the fact that most of them were dark-haired and an occasional sentence in Spanish dropped into the conversation, they were as smartly dressed and sophisticated-looking as any group of young high school or college graduates. Their smiles were welcoming as Dr. Jim made the introductions. Although Betty was several years younger, it was obvious that they were ready to accept her. "We're having a meeting at my house next Friday," a girl named Lola told her. "We'd love to have you come."

"I'm terribly sorry," Betty blurted hastily, remembering the invitation from Laurel. Before she could continue her explanation she was interrupted by a burst of fanfare.

Dick mounted the bandstand. He announced that the dance had been a great success; over three hundred dollars had been netted for the Gabriel Delgado Memorial Fund. Final disposition of the money had not been decided, but Dick promised that it would be something fitting, ". . . . so we won't forget."

The audience stood at attention as the overhead lights slowly dimmed. Head bowed, Betty joined the others for that hushed moment of remembrance. "So we won't forget," she repeated softly.

Then the lights came on again and the band struck the warning strains of the final number. Betty saw Agnes, Laurel, and Babs crossing the floor toward her. With a quick good-by to Dr. Jim and his friends, she rushed to join them. "We've been looking everywhere for you," Agnes scolded, taking Betty's arm. "We're going to duck out on the last dance. It's the only way we'll ever get seats at the Black-and-Gold."

On the other side, Laurel had taken Betty's arm too. Once again it swept over her: that warm, sweet feeling of really belonging. Only Babs glanced back at the group in the corner. "Who are those people you were talking to?"

Betty caught Babs' slightly lifted eyebrows. "Oh, nobody," she replied hastily. "Just nobody at all."

14

Merry Christmas, Everybody!

"Oh, Dick, it sounds divine! No, it isn't too late. I'd love to go." Inside her white moccasins, Betty's toes curled with anticipation; she hugged the phone closer to her ear. "I mean . . . of course, I'll have to ask my mother."

"I'll wait. Tell her it's going to be a big party." Even across the telephone wires Dick's voice seemed to share that same excitement.

Pattering across the dining room, Betty flung open the kitchen door. Mrs. Ochoa looked up from where she had been forming a wreath with some bright-berried native holly. "What's this . . . an invitation?" It was impossible not to have overheard, with the telephone just around the corner in the next room.

"Yes, Mamma, it's Dick. He's invited me to a party at Babs Sutherland's house tonight, a simply wonderful Christmas party!"

"Tonight?" Mrs. Ochoa gasped. "But it's only two days until Christmas. Tonight is *Los Posadas*."

"Oh, Mamma, that's just for children!" Betty's voice was exasperated. "This is a real grown-up party. Babs' folks have even hired an orchestra. Imagine that!"

If Mrs. Ochoa wanted to imagine someone being wealthy enough to hire an orchestra for a young people's party, there was no sign of it in the sudden tightening around her mouth. "You have never missed a *Los Posadas*, Betty—not since the first one when you were just a baby and I carried you in my arms."

There was an angry kink in Betty's chest. "Just because I've always gone before doesn't mean I can't change!" she charged. "It isn't like it was Christmas Eve. We'll all attend Mass together tomorrow night. Even Father Gargan admits there isn't the interest there used to be—that's why they're celebrating *Los Posadas* just one night this year instead of the usual nine. People have other things to do at Christmastime nowadays!"

"Christmas is a time for your family and your church," her mother replied stonily. "You simply cannot go to the party. I have already promised Father Gargan that you will help with the children." Her lips settled into the firm line of determination that told Betty the conversation was closed.

Helpless with frustration, Betty returned to the phone. "I can't go, Dick." It was all she could do to hold back the tears. "My mother won't let me. There's some program at the church."

"I see." Dick's voice was disappointed too. "I'm sorry,

Betty." He hesitated, then apparently finding no further topic of conversation, he ended the call. "Well, have a Merry Christmas and Happy New Year. I'll be seeing you at school."

"Merry Christmas," Betty choked in a small voice and she replaced the receiver. For a second it didn't seem as if she could bear the disappointment, the salty tears that stung her eyes. As though this first week of Christmas vacation hadn't been dull enough, with both Pam and Agnes out of town visiting relatives! "I'll be seeing you at school." That meant Dick wasn't going to ask her for another date during vacation. How could her parents be so old-fashioned!

With lagging footsteps she returned to the kitchen where she had been washing the breakfast dishes before the important call. Mrs. Ochoa glanced up from the now-finished and very professional-looking wreath. "I'm sorry, dear . . . maybe if it had been for some time next week . . . But it seems very late for a young man to be asking for a date. You know I am right. Christmas *is* important."

Without a word Betty let a plate slide into the cottony suds. Important—if only her mother knew how important! She didn't care if it was late and Dick had probably asked someone else first. That wonderful party at Laurel's four weeks ago, now this invitation to Babs'. To have to turn down an invitation just when she was beginning to be accepted by the best crowd at school! It was unfair.

Betty's stormy mood continued throughout the day. Even the festive Christmas preparations, which she usually enjoyed so much, failed to revive her spirits. Gloomily she helped Larry string red berries to add to the already decorated tree in the living room, joined Gloria in arranging fresh candles and sprays of holly around the plaster figures of the little crèche on the sideboard.

After dinner that night Mrs. Ochoa helped Gloria into her costume: a full green skirt, a richly embroidered blouse, a flowing mantle to cover her hair. It might not be authentic but it was the nearest they could come to what the women of Bethlehem might have worn on that Holy night nearly two thousand years ago. Betty remembered years past when she had dressed with equal enthusiasm. But tonight she just slipped a warm coat over her skirt and sweater as she joined the others in the car.

At the church, some twenty or thirty children were already milling about the steps, while a handful of adults tried to straighten them into line. Most of the children were in costumes: some elaborate and detailed like Gloria's; others makeshift like Larry's, an old cape for a robe, a bright-colored towel wound into a turban. First came the young boy and girl who would enact the part of Mary and Joseph, then the wise men, behind them the carolers and the other children.

Someone jostled Betty's arm. She saw with a start that it was Dr. Jim. His white shirt was rumpled and he had a slightly harried look as he balanced three flat boxes in his arms. "Am I glad to see you!" He thrust a box into her hands. "Here, those tykes at the end don't have their candles yet. See if you can get them into line. And for heavens' sake, try to keep them quiet!"

Passing out candles, readjusting a mantilla that was about to slide off, tying a small shoelace, pushing first one tiny figure, then another, into position, Betty had no time for thoughts, gloomy or otherwise. Then almost miraculously there was silence, everyone in place, every candle lit. A brief word from Father Gargan and the procession was under way, the high, sweet voices of the carolers filling the night air.

As Betty with the half-dozen grownups fell into place at the rear, Dr. Jim joined her. "Here, you forgot your candle." His dark eyes reflecting the sparkle of his own white taper, he lit another for her. Several cars slowed on the street, curious motorists turning to stare. "What if some of the crowd on the way to Babs' party should come by and see me now?" the miserable thought flashed through Betty's mind.

Their first stop was two doors beyond the church, at the home of old Mrs. Para. Betty remembered years ago, attending her catechism classes at Señora Para's house. The elderly woman and her two middle-aged daughters were already waiting on the porch. In reply to the traditional plea for shelter, her face twisted in mock anger and she made the sign that there was no room for the Holy Family in her small abode.

As the procession re-formed and went back through the gate, Mrs. Para and her daughters locked their house behind them and joined the end of the line. Betty and Dr. Jim paused long enough to give them candles too.

At six other houses the little band stopped to make their plea for admission; at each they received the answer that there was no room. They had reached the business section of Meridian Avenue now. Though most of the small stores were closed for the night, the street was gay with their Christmas decorations. El Tipo Café could hardly be considered a *posada* or inn, but as far back as Betty could remember, out of respect for Señor and Señora Moreno, it always had been one of their stops. There was the scratchy wail of the juke box being hurriedly turned off, while those inside gathered respectfully in the doorway. When the procession started on again, Betty was surprised to see that a half-dozen or more had joined them, among them Benny Ruiz and several other boys from *Los Coyotes*.

A block beyond El Tipo Café, the party turned off on a darkened side street that crossed the railroad tracks and led through the vacant fields beyond the old orange-packing plant. By now so many had joined the procession, it was nearly a block long. Suddenly in the crisp, cold darkness, lit only by the wavering glow of many small candles, Betty was aware of a tugging emotion in her heart. It was the same sweet, half-joyous, half-solemn feeling she had known as a child. How beautiful it was! How could she ever have called *Los Posadas* old-fashioned? She could hear Gloria's voice, sweet and true, soaring above all the others. Could "Silent Night, Holy Night" ever be more beautiful than when it was sung in Spanish? It took the rich, musical flow of the language to give it true meaning.

On their right they passed the sprawling, dark shadows of the Almansor Street School. But ahead, the old warehouse that now served as the Youth Center was ablaze with lights. Betty recognized her mother among those in the doorway. Already the children's faces were kindling, their footsteps speeding with anticipation. This time there was no refusal; the party swept inside joyfully. For a few minutes they knelt in prayer before the figures of the Nativity tableau set up on a long table. Then Father Gargan motioned them to rise. The solemnity was over; it was time for the party to begin.

Someone started a lively melody on the phonograph and organized a dancing game. It was hard to keep the children's attention on games. Already their eyes were going to the *piñata* hanging from the ceiling. Some of the bolder youngsters were leaping into the air, trying to touch it with their hands. Betty had to admit it was one of the biggest *piñatas* she had ever seen, looking like a huge, suspended beehive, its thin clay shell decorated with ribbons and tinsel . . . and inside? Well, wasn't that the whole thrill of a *piñata*, wondering what was inside?

Dr. Jim put his hands over his ears and grimaced at the bedlam. "All right, all right," a man's voice called. "We'll have the *piñata* now."

A small boy was blindfolded and armed with a broomstick. On his first swing he missed the *piñata* by three feet; on his second he charged into the crowd, several shrieking girls scattering in front of him. The next to try was a little girl. It didn't matter that she was so short she couldn't hope to break the *piñata*. She swung the stick with such vigor that it would have cracked the head of a little boy if Benny Ruiz hadn't snatched him to safety just in time. By now Betty was laughing so hard her sides ached.

When it was Larry's turn, Betty saw him take a careful bearing before the blindfold was fastened in place. His first blow grazed the edge and sent the *piñata* swinging. The children let out a shriek of delight. "Come on, Larry!" Betty screamed with the others, jumping up and down. With the next blow there was a cracking, shattering sound as the shell burst, candies, suckers, little wrapped prizes flying in every direction, while the children in a squirming mass of legs and arms dove to scoop them up. Betty couldn't resist scrambling for a few herself. She was just dumping them into the hands of a starry-eyed little toddler who had been too shy to join the others when she saw Dr. Jim watching her. "Why, Miss Ochoa, I didn't know you were one of the *muchachas*?" he teased.

As the hubbub subsided, Mrs. Moreno appeared in the

doorway to the small kitchen at the end of the hall. "*Vaya!*" she called. "I need help. The ice cream, it melts."

Betty crowded into the kitchen with her mother, Mrs. Moreno, and several other women. Her hands flew, dishing ice cream into the paper cups, while Dr. Jim and the other men distributed it among the children.

At nine o'clock it was over, the party broke up. Some of the children were still singing as they left. Smaller ones, already drowsy, were carried on their parents' shoulders. As Betty went to look for Larry's costume, she saw Dr. Jim talking to her mother. At first her mother seemed to be hesitating about something; then she was smiling and bobbing her head. As Betty joined them, playfully slamming Larry's costume over his small head, Dr. Jim smiled at her. "Some of us are going to another party at a friend's house down the street. Your mother says you can come if you like."

Betty swung to her mother wonderingly. "You mean it's all right . . . ?"

Mrs. Ochoa nodded. "I think so . . . maybe just this one time." She didn't have to say more, the sudden softness in her dark eyes told Betty the rest. It was because of what had happened that morning; she had known the disappointment that had been in her daughter's heart. But as Mrs. Ochoa started for the door with Gloria and Larry, she looked back, her lips settling again in that firm line. "Remember, Dr. Sanchez, she must be home at twelve."

Since it was Dr. Jim's responsibility to lock the hall, they were the last to leave. Betty took one last, dismayed look behind her: the floor littered with paper streamers, empty ice cream cups, candy wrappers . . . someone would have a terrible job tomorrow. As though he had read her mind,

Dr. Jim clicked the lock in place and shrugged his shoulders. "*Mañana* . . ."

Betty gave a delicious giggle and shrugged also. "*Mañana*," she echoed. It was a nice feeling. Sometimes it did you good to shrug responsibilities behind and live just for the moment.

When they reached Dr. Jim's car, Betty was surprised to see Benny Ruiz and Jenny Lopez waiting for them. "Hop in, kids, we're late already," Dr. Jim told them. Betty sat in the middle while Jenny, with a shy little smile, eased onto Benny's lap. She sat very prim and stiff. "What's wrong?" Benny growled. "I don't bite." Betty noticed that he gave her a little squeeze as he said it.

Dr. Jim chuckled. "He's right, Jenny. I think these *Coyotes* do more howling and barking than they do biting."

"Darn you, doc," Benny grumbled. "Now you've spoiled my reputation!" Everyone laughed.

As Dr. Jim had said, their destination was only a block away. It was a small house, much more modest than Betty's home. But she noticed the fence was neatly whitewashed and as they came up the walk, in spite of its being late December, there was the spicy smell of geraniums in the air. When the door opened, she recognized Lola, the girl whom she had met at the dance. "Dr. Jim, Betty, Benny, Jenny . . . I'm glad you could come," she said.

Inside, there were fifteen or sixteen other young people whom Betty recognized as members of *Los Hildagos*. Though the room was small, the rugs had been taken up and some were dancing, while others talked or wandered back and forth. Caught in a threesome just coming out of the kitchen, Betty was separated from Dr. Jim. When she looked around she couldn't see him anywhere. She made her way across the room and sank onto what appeared to be the only vacant seat, on one corner of the sofa.

"*Hola.* What are you doing here?"

For a second Betty hardly recognized the young man beside her. Without the leather jacket that was his trademark, in a neatly pressed blue suit and white shirt, Pete looked completely different.

"Why, Pete, I didn't expect to see you here either." Betty's voice bubbled with relief. At least it was nice to see someone her own age, someone she had spoken to a few more times than just a hasty introduction at a dance. "It's a nice party, isn't it?" she added.

Pete shrugged. "Okay, I guess." Then his face flushed. "I mean it's real nice. Want a Coke?"

"Not now. I just came from *Los Posadas.* We had a lot to eat there."

Pete scowled at the tips of his shoes, polished to such a sheen that they caught the reflection of the overhead lights. "I didn't go this year. My little sister went though."

"Well, I can tell you she did all right then." Betty laughed. "Such a *piñata*! I never saw one so big." The laughter died and an uncomfortable silence returned. Couldn't Pete say anything?

Then his head bobbed up. "Since you don't want a Coke, do you want to dance?"

Grinning with relief, Betty sprang to her feet. There wasn't any need for conversation, dancing with Pete. He was a good dancer. They danced perfectly together, as though the quick beat of the music reached their feet with the same joyous abandon. Abruptly the music stopped. There was a rustling and shoving. When it started again, Betty found herself dancing with another partner, a short, pleasant-faced man of about twenty-five. "I'm Rudy," he introduced himself. "I met you at the Home-coming Dance." Before they could pursue the conversation further, the music stopped again and there was another scramble. This time it was Benny who took Betty in his arms. He was a good dancer also, but too wild for her taste with his crazy, impossible steps. However, as a bobby pin jerked loose and her hair tumbled about her face, she found herself laughing.

There wasn't any pairing off at this dance, any chance to be a wallflower. Suddenly someone would stop the record and there would be a mad rush to exchange partners. There wasn't time to be bored, or worried, or even to struggle with conversation if you didn't happen to know your partner very well. Yet most often it seemed to be Pete who was right there, seizing Betty's arm, grabbing her shoulder, as the music stopped. It was such fun that she forgot all about Dr. Jim's disappearance.

Suddenly the phonograph stopped for good. Outside, there was a heavy tromping on the front porch. "Ho, ho, ho! Merry Christmas, everybody."

A short, enormously padded Santa Claus stood in the doorway. "Ho, ho, ho! Merry Christmas, boys and girls!" In spite of the false beard and pillow-stuffed figure, there was no mistaking Dr. Jim. That gusty, booming laugh was a give-away.

Santa Claus threw down his bag. "Step right up, folks. Presents for the boys and girls. First let's take our hostess."

Smiling, Lola stepped forward. Then she let out a little shriek as a strong arm pulled her close and a resounding kiss was pressed against her cheek. "Ho, ho, ho—one of the privileges of being Santa." Everyone burst into laughter as their eyes raised to the sprig of mistletoe above Dr. Jim's head.

"Come on, girls. Come on, don't be shy," he beckoned. Several of the girls came forward. Some managed to duck in time; some were caught for a kiss as everyone laughed. "I get to be Santa next year!" Rudy insisted.

Then it was Betty's turn. She tried to grab her present and run, but Dr. Jim was too quick for her. "Ho, ho, ho, one of the wee ones," he chuckled as he planted a fatherly kiss on her cheek. There was a sudden movement in the crowd as Pete darted forward.

"Hold her! She's still under the mistletoe!" A muscular brown hand pinioned Betty's arm. But she struggled frantically, ducking just in time. She and Pete both landed across the room, panting as they leaned against the wall, their laughter joining that of the others.

Betty's cheeks were crimson. But she wasn't really angry. How could she be? Standing together, a good, safe distance from the mistletoe, she and Pete unwrapped their gifts. Pete's was a key chain, hers a tiny bottle of perfume, the kind that can be bought in any dime store. But it wasn't the gift itself; it was the idea behind it. Everyone had received something.

When Santa had emptied his bag and disappeared into the bedroom to get out of the bundlesome clothes, Lola motioned from the kitchen doorway. Everyone formed a line and filed into the kitchen where Lola, her husband, and another woman served them crisp, hot *tacos*.

Betty and Pete found a place near the phonograph where they could enjoy theirs. "Good," Pete commented through a mouthful.

Betty nodded, her mouth too scorched to answer. These

were real Mexican *tacos*, not the dull, tamed-down kind you bought in restaurants. Along with the tears they brought to her eyes was a glow that reached to her toe tips.

"Do you belong to *Los Hildagos*? I mean do you come to all these parties?" It was Pete's first real effort at conversation.

Betty shook her head. "No. Tonight's my first time."

Pete glanced down at his shoes. "First time for me too."

Betty looked down at her feet too; one slipper traced a pattern on the floor. It was a crazy thought, so crazy it made her cheeks turn pink. She wished now that she hadn't struggled so hard back there under the mistletoe. Well, really, it was just in fun! And wouldn't it have been nicer to have someone young like Pete kiss her than . . . practically an old man like Dr. Jim? Then finding Pete staring at her intently, she blushed harder than ever. She hoped he wasn't a mind-reader.

All too soon it was midnight, the party over. Outside by his car, Dr. Jim offered to give Pete a ride home. Benny and Jenny had gone with another couple. Pete hesitated a moment, then his shoulders hunched and something of the old belligerence seemed to return. "No, thanks . . . it's only a little way." He started down the street alone, then abruptly he turned and his white grin flashed in the darkness. "Merry Christmas, Betty."

"Well, did you have a good time?" Dr. Jim asked. Betty looked out the window at the bright decorations still shining from the little stores along Meridian Avenue. They passed the dark shadow of the church with the lighted Nativity scene on the lawn, the same *Nacimiento* that had been there every year since Betty was a tiny girl.

"A wonderful time, Dr. Jim," she said slowly. And she knew that she meant every word of it. *Los Posadas*, Santa

Claus, ice cream, *tacos*, getting to know Pete a little better . . . who could have asked for a better Christmas? Maybe even more important than the fun she'd had tonight was a sudden new idea that had come to her—a wonderful new idea that was going to help everyone at Bellamar!

15

Traitor!

Wednesday afternoon after the reopening of school, Betty could hardly wait to get downstairs from Mr. Mead's lab to the council room. It had been difficult keeping her idea a secret, especially from Agnes who had returned from vacation brimming with questions. But Betty told herself that her plan was too important to be shared anywhere outside of council meeting.

This last week, as she had mulled it over in her mind, an even more dazzling thought had come to her. If she was successful in putting over a project of such size, she might very well be a candidate for the "most outstanding senior" award in June. She knew the last was a selfish thought.

But what student didn't dream of that most coveted of awards? Dick, Dave, Agnes—all probably had the same ambition.

Dick was already seated at the long table when Betty entered. As she slipped into her place and opened the red binder, she flashed him an enthusiastic smile. "Put me down for new business, Dick. I came up with an idea over vacation, a really big idea that could solve all our problems."

Dick straightened from where he had been sorting his notes. "Really? Good girl, Betts, I knew I could count on you for something!" His eyes said that he would like to hear more, but already the others were filing into the room. In addition to the twelve regular council members, there were a half-dozen committee chairmen who were to give reports. Among them was Agnes. Betty tossed her a welcoming grin as she bent to review her notes for what must have been the hundredth time.

Because of vacation, the ordinary routine of the meeting seemed to take an unusually long time: correction of the minutes, a string of committee reports, a haggle over a minor problem of old business. Only fifteen minutes were left of the hour when Dick announced that the meeting was open for new business. Then without waiting for a show of hands, he motioned to Betty that she had the floor.

Eyes sparkling, Betty got to her feet. "It's an absolutely wonderful idea!" Coloring with embarrassment, she amended quickly, "I mean, *I* think it's a marvelous idea. You all know what a success we made of the Gabriel Delgado Memorial Dance. I think we're all agreed that the improvement of relations between English- and Spanish-speaking students at Bellamar High School is one of our major problems this year."

She paused importantly. "Well, during vacation I attended a party given by an organization of young Spanish-speaking people called *Los Hildagos*. They're a wonderful group. They do charity work, like donating time and equipment to the Youth Center. But mostly they are a social organization, giving dances, parties, having fun together. The only trouble with *Los Hildagos* is that they're all adults, in their twenties and early thirties."

Again Betty waited, seeing the nods of interest. "What I suggest is that we form a club here at school patterned after *Los Hildagos*, only a club for Spanish-speaking students. It would be school-sponsored, school-controlled. With a special organization of their own, there wouldn't be any need for gangs and the Mexican students would have a real part in school activities. I've even thought of a name," Betty concluded. "In-Betweeners. In-Betweeners, representing the transition between the old and the new."

Babs was the first to speak. "Why, Betty, it is a wonderful idea!"

"It's super!" Agnes burst out impulsively, even though she was only a spectator.

"I think so too," someone else chimed in.

Betty looked down the table to Dick. He was staring at the papers in front of him, a strange, puckery frown between his eyes. His pencil scribbled on the corner of a note pad. "I agree with Betty that something needs to be done to encourage the Spanish-speaking students to take a more active part in campus life." The pencil stopped and he looked up, gray eyes meeting Betty's bluntly. "But, Betty, I don't agree with this idea of a special club at all. I think you're going at the problem the wrong way. To put the Spanish-speaking students in a club of their own wouldn't make them more a part of student affairs—it would be separating them even further! Besides, we already have a Spanish Club."

Betty was aware of a sudden thickness in her throat. She couldn't believe that she had heard Dick correctly. Why she'd counted on his support . . . they'd always worked together!

"Dick, you don't understand," she exclaimed impatiently. "Of course we have a Spanish Club, for students who take Spanish. But this would be a club for Spanish-speaking students, students of Mexican descent."

Dick's eyes were cold. "I understand all right. That's just what I don't like. Spanish Club is for students who study Spanish. Science Club is for students who like Science. Beaux Arts is for artists. They're organizations based on mutual interests. What you're suggesting is a club founded on racial lines!"

Betty could feel the anger swelling in her throat. "Dick, that's not true, I just . . ."

"Please, I still have the floor!" Dick interrupted brusquely. "Just how would you draw the membership of this organization? Spanish-speaking, you say? Well, Morrie here has spent two summers in Mexico; does that make him a member? I struggled through two years of Spanish—am I a member too? Aren't you really suggesting a club that isn't for Spanish-speaking students but for students whose hair happens to be a little blacker, whose skin is a little darker, whose parents happened to have been born in a foreign country? It's downright segregation!"

Then, as though he was aware the situation was becoming too tense, Dick's eyes twinkled. "If we're going to start clubs on that basis, how about putting Agnes and Babs and Bill here in a club of their own—just for carrot-tops?"

Someone snickered. Betty failed to catch the intended

easing note of humor. All she caught was the sarcasm. For Dick—of all people—to make fun of her! "You aren't even trying to understand," she snapped furiously.

"I still like the idea," Babs interposed. "I think we should take a vote."

Dick glanced at the clock. "I'm afraid there isn't time. This meeting should have been over ten minutes ago. I suggest we talk about it next week." Before Betty could jump to her feet, Dave Riordan was ahead of her. "I move that the meeting be adjourned."

"Second the motion."

"But we haven't talked about my idea, we haven't . . ." Betty sputtered.

Dick called for a vote. The motion carried by a small margin and the meeting was over. As Betty gathered her books she was trembling. Her fingers were so clumsy that papers spilled from the binder; the zipper wouldn't close.

As she started for the door, Dick glanced up. "I'm sorry, Betty," he said briefly. "I promise we'll take it up next week. Meanwhile you think about it."

"Sorry!" Betty gasped. Suddenly she was unable to control the seething rage of pain and rebuff. "Sorry! Talk about railroading. They said you had a way of running things to suit yourself. I didn't believe them—but I sure do now! You . . . you traitor!"

As she flounced through the doorway, cheeks burning, she heard a voice behind her. "I told you if those two ever tangled there'd be some real fireworks."

"Yeah," someone giggled. "I think the irresistible object just chunked into the immovable object."

Betty's cheeks singed even hotter. In the hall, it was all Agnes' long legs could do to keep up with her. "Hey, slow down, will you? I'm out of breath."

Betty slowed slightly. Already she was ashamed of her display of temper, but she still was angry. "I was a little rough, wasn't I?" she admitted.

Agnes wiped her forehead. "Rough? Honey child, when you get mad you go off like a firecracker." Then grinning, she linked her arm through the smaller girl's. "Let's go over to the Black-and-Gold. My treat. A Coke will cool you off."

But even sitting in the quiet booth, sipping her cherry Coke, Betty couldn't push back the anger. For Dick to have turned against her so . . . it was almost more than she could bear!

Agnes leaned across the table. "Now get me straight, Betty, I like Dick. Everyone likes him. But you have to admit he does like to run the whole show." She took a long, noisy sip of her Coke and gave Betty a loyal smile. "If you ask me, I bet Dick really does like the idea. The trouble is that you thought of it first. Dick just can't stand someone else coming up with a really good idea."

Betty's spirits brightened a little. "You mean that, Agnes?"

"You bet I mean it. Dick isn't the whole council anyhow. You have plenty of supporters."

"I don't know . . ." Betty's voice was dubious.

"Look"—Agnes nudged her—"you'll see."

Babs had come through the door of the Black-and-Gold. She looked around for a moment, then her feet brought her straight to the booth where the two girls were sitting.

"Mind if I join you?" she asked, dropping into the space next to Agnes. She picked up a menu casually, then across the top her eyes caught Betty's. "Darling, you really stirred up a hornet's nest. You notice I am minus my best friend, Laurel? If I'm not mistaken she's with Dick, helping him lick his wounds. And I can tell you he has plenty!"

Betty stiffened. Somehow the thought of Laurel comforting Dick wasn't particularly appealing. But Babs, having made herself comfortable, was already continuing. "I'm on your side, Betty. I think you've come up with the best idea anyone's had all year. You wait, we'll push it through without Dick's support."

"You're serious, Babs? You really like the idea?" Betty urged.

"Like it?" Babs laughed. "It's just about the smartest idea I've heard. After all, it's time we did something to keep those Mexicans in their place."

Betty set her Coke down abruptly. Keep the Mexicans in their place? But that hadn't been her idea at all!

Babs had ordered a sundae now. Between dips, she and Agnes were deep in conversation. Betty's straw stirred the last half-inch of Coke in her glass. She couldn't finish it. The flavor was gone. Could that be how the others had taken her suggestion too? Could it be that somehow Dick was right after all . . . and that her wonderful new idea for the In-Betweeners Club was all wrong?

16

Good Neighbors

Betty wished that Babs had not made that chance remark at the Black-and-Gold. The next week, even when she was at her happiest puttering in the art room after school, sharing cups of hot chocolate with Pam and Agnes in the Barnes' cozy kitchen, the memory returned like a persistent mosquito buzzing through her mind. Was this plan for the In-Betweeners Club not a sound one? Or was it just the dread of another battle with Dick that had tarnished her shining enthusiasm?

Wednesday morning, instead of bouncing out of bed with the usual zest that greeted the most exciting day of the week, Betty arose with a leaden feeling that matched the gloomy, overcast sky outside the window. "You're working too hard," Mrs. Ochoa scolded worriedly at the breakfast table. "All this rushing around, all these activities—they are too much!"

'Oh, Mamma, I never felt better in my life!" Betty shifted fretfully under the too-knowing gaze. "Nothing's wrong. Nothing at all." But the listless way she poked at the eggs in front of her made a lie of the words. Settled roundly in their whites, the eggs were two yellow-pupiled eyes staring knowingly too.

"I still don't like it," Mrs. Ochoa persisted. "Every afternoon some meeting after school, some new project. When I was in school, just keeping up with my studies was enough."

For a moment Betty tried to imagine what it must have been like when her mother was a girl, living with Grandmother Ortega, who was so old-fashioned and strict, who always wore a black *rebozo* on the street, who still refused to trade at the big super-market, preferring the same small neighborhood store where red *chiles* hung from the ceiling and pale, freckled tortillas were stacked in fresh piles each morning. Abruptly Betty laid down her fork. Why hadn't she thought of it before? Her mother had attended a big high school. Like many of the students from Meridian Avenue, her mother had been second-generation too!

"Tell me something, Mamma." Betty's eyes glowed with eagerness. "When you were in school, how would you have liked it if someone had started a special club just for the Mexican-American students, a big club where you could make new friends?"

"A club for Mexican students?" Mrs. Ochoa rested the coffee pot against the sink as she pondered the question. "But I already knew the Mexican students. We lived in the same neighborhood, we attended the same church, we traded at the same stores. Oh no, I wouldn't have cared for a club like that!" She tossed her head as she poured a cup of coffee. "Why would I have needed more Mexican friends? It was the others who were hard to know."

Betty stared down at her plate while her mother's words dropped into her mind, like pebbles sinking to the bottom of a pond. Why, indeed? How could she have been so blind! Carried away by the excitement of the Christmas party, in her desire to do something big, she hadn't stopped to consider how the Mexican students themselves might feel about such a club. There were probably no people on earth more openhearted and gregarious than the Mexican people. Just the immense Sunday gatherings at her own home should have told her that. What advantage would there be for them in a club where they knew everyone already? How would that make new friends? It would isolate them even further, make them feel even less welcome to join the other school activities. If she hadn't been such a hothead, so stubborn, she would have seen it from the beginning.

"Oh, Mamma, thank you!" Betty gasped through a final mouthful.

"Thank me?" Mrs. Ochoa's face was bewildered. But Betty had already snatched her raincoat. She blew a kiss from the doorway. "Have to rush. Tell you about it tonight!"

By the time Betty reached the end of Paloma Road, that first joyous release that comes from making a right decision had vanished. Her footsteps slowed as the miserable weight returned. Realizing you had made a mistake was one thing. But admitting it in front of the whole Student Council was another—especially after the scene she had made last week!

She already had a reputation for temper. Now she would have one for being a scatterbrain. And with abandonment of the plans for the In-Betweeners would go her dream of the outstanding senior award.

For a second the thought came to her that she didn't have to speak up: there was still a chance the project would be voted down in council meeting. She could remain quiet and wait for the vote. But even as the thought sneaked through her mind, she recognized it as cowardice.

By noon it had begun to rain, one of those slashing California downpours that filled the quad with puddles and swept under the runways. Students darting between buildings hugged their books and ran with lowered heads. Eating lunch in the shelter of the overcrowded cafeteria, Betty had no chance to discuss her decision with Agnes. Her only hope was to catch Dick before the start of the council meeting.

But when the final bell sounded that afternoon, Mr. Mead asked her to remain after class. As though it wasn't bad enough having two physics papers returned as incomplete, by the time Betty reached the student offices, the council members were already in their seats. Was it her imagination or did Dick turn away purposely to avoid even a nod of greeting? Wilted as the soggy branches whipping outside the window, Betty sank into her chair.

How quickly that meeting proceeded compared to the one of the week before! There were no corrections of the minutes, only one committee report. Then Dick was rapping his gavel to open the discussion of old business. "Formation of a club for students of Latin parentage—Betty Ochoa has the floor."

As Betty rose to her feet, faces turned expectantly. She knew what they were thinking. This was going to be it, the battle royal. "Mr. President, members of the council . . . Last week I made a proposal for the formation of a club for students of Mexican descent at Bellamar High School. With your permission I'd like to withdraw that proposal at this time."

There was a moment of stunned silence. Babs looked as if someone had doused her with ice water; even Dick was blinking. Betty swallowed a walnut-sized lump in her throat and hurried on:

"I know I was the one who made the suggestion and withdrawing it must sound crazy. But I've had time to think these last few days and I realize now that I was wrong. Such a club might be fine outside of school. But Dick was right; it doesn't have any place in our school organization. Our problem isn't getting the Mexican-American students better acquainted with each other, it's getting them better acquainted with us. Four years ago most of us gave up our Hawes Street and Northridge rivalries to become a united student body. Now we need to encourage the Mexican-Americans to break up their rivalries and gangs to become a part of the school too. I not only want to withdraw my suggestion"—Betty stumbled over the conclusion—"I guess I should apologize to Dick for losing my temper."

The room was so quiet you could hear the muffled tap of the radiator. Someone cleared his throat. But if Betty had imagined it would be the most horrible experience of her life, meeting Dick's eyes for that second of apology, she was wrong. Hardly had she slumped back to her seat than Dick was on his feet, gray eyes aimed directly at her.

"Thanks, Betty. I think we all agree: a speech like that takes spunk. And I still don't think your suggestion was entirely bad—at least you came up with an idea, which is more than anyone else can say. In fact, I think we've all been making exactly the same mistake. Since the hard feeling that followed Gabriel Delgado's death, we've all been trying too hard, pushing too fast. Some of us have less than a year left at Bellamar. We wanted to come up with something big, some revolutionary change that would solve our problem overnight. Well, maybe some problems aren't solved that easily. The Gabriel Delgado Dance was one small step forward. Maybe we should be content with just another small step. What Betty said about our old Hawes Street and Northridge rivalries has given me an idea. How many of us lost those animosities overnight? For most of us it started with the making of just one new friendship, discovering just one student who wasn't so bad after all."

Betty nodded eagerly. She remembered that day as a freshman when she and Agnes collided in the hall. After brushing each other off and making apologies, they'd discovered they had two classes together, they both thought Mr. Heatherington was an old grouch, Miss Potter a living dream . . .

Dick leaned forward, gripping the table. "There are twelve of us here. Each of us is prominent in at least one after-school activity. These next months, if each of us would make it his personal obligation to invite just one student of Mexican descent to join his club, and later this student could invite another . . ."

"You mean like Betty's election posters!" Morrie interrupted. "Someone starts the movement and then it keeps growing and growing."

"I know a kid who is a sharp auto mechanic. I could get him into the 'Hot-Rodders,' " Dave added.

"Just a minute—hold on!" Dick held up his hands. His eyes had that crinkly look as they met Betty's. "Let's not go overboard again. Besides, Betty's supposed to have the monopoly on enthusiasm around here. It won't be that easy. Just inviting a student to join your club won't be enough. You'll have to make friends with him, stick with him until he becomes a real part of the organization, see that he's promoted to an office or committee chairmanship. Even then there will be failures. But by the end of the year, if we have created just a small nucleus of twelve Mexican-Americans who are student leaders, we will have made a beginning."

It was such a simple idea—so simple compared to Betty's elaborate scheme—that she wondered how they had overlooked it before. Hardly had the unanimous vote been taken to follow Dick's proposal when Babs' hand shot into the air. "I have another suggestion. In the spring we have our annual carnival. Usually it's a Mardi Gras; but there's nothing in the rules that says it has to follow the Mardi Gras theme. This year why don't we make the carnival a Fiesta?"

"With Mexican food . . . *taco, enchiladas*!" someone added.

It didn't seem possible that the meeting which had threatened to become a battleground could suddenly have turned into the most enthusiastic they had ever had. Even when the session had been adjourned, they lingered. It was only the arrival of the janitor that scattered them into the halls.

At her locker, Betty put away all of her books except the physics text. As she bounded back up the stairs, she saw Carmen Ortiz coming out of the attendance office.

"Carmen, wait. I'll walk with you," she called.

Startled, the tall girl with the dark pompadour spun around. Then the cool mask of pretended indifference dropped into place again. She shrugged. "Okay. But if you're selling some kind of tickets, I can't buy any today."

Betty told herself that she deserved that sudden jab in her heart. Years ago she and Carmen had attended the same catechism class; though Carmen was only a junior, they had several classes together. Yet how much interest had she shown in Carmen in high school, outside of a hasty nod in the hall or trying to sell her tickets to something? "It isn't tickets today." Betty forced a weak smile. "I wanted to talk to you. You do such wonderful art work, I was wondering why you never joined Beaux Arts?"

Carmen shrugged again. "I don't have much time. None of my friends belong . . ."

Betty knew the first wasn't true. Carmen didn't belong to any school clubs; she spent her afternoons in El Tipo Café. "But I'm your friend and I belong!" Betty insisted. "Besides, I need your help. You know I'm chairman of the Decorations Committee. Next month we start the posters for the carnival. You do such beautiful poster work I was hoping you would join the club and by my assistant."

For the first time there was a crack in that haughty composure. "Well, if you really need the help . . ." Carmen's voice was condescending as she clung to that last precious shred of pride. Then unable to hide the sudden sparkle lighting her dark eyes, she seized Betty's arm. "What kind of posters are we going to make?"

They had reached the front steps now. Betty was surprised to see that the rain had stopped. The sun, breaking through a rift in the clouds, bathed everything with glistening newness. The gray buildings looked as if they had been newly painted; the winter-browned grass had recaptured a shadow of green, while the palm fronds glistened with a million raindrop diamonds. She took one last look at the physics book tucked under her arm. If she worked very hard she could finish those papers tonight. "Come on, let's stop by the Black-and-Gold and have a Coke, Carmen. My treat. We have plans to make!"

Carmen's voice was hesitant. "It's a little out of our way . . ."

"Okay. El Tipo then!" Betty grinned happily as they locked arms.

17

La Fiesta

If Betty had encountered no difficulty in persuading Carmen to join Beaux Arts, it was not that easy for the others in those ensuing weeks. Years of indifference, outright resentment such as had followed the Delgado incident, could not be erased overnight. But Babs finally found a part for talented Jenny Verdugo in the school operetta, Dave enticed Tony Moreno into the Hot-Rodders. Oddly enough, it was Dick who had the most difficult time. For some reason he had chosen Pete Flores as his candidate. But early in March, when Pete turned out for baseball, he brought two other members of *Los Coyotes* with him.

The movement seemed so small, sometimes Betty

wanted to explode with impatience. But deep in her heart she knew Dick had been right. Some problems can't be solved overnight. And as the weeks and then the first months of spring slipped by, there seemed to be a lessening of tension and a new friendliness in the halls at school.

One Monday in May, as Betty and Agnes joined the others in the cafeteria, they found them discussing still another problem that had remained unsolved. With all their activities and the heavy burden of schoolwork, they had almost forgotten the Gabriel Delgado Memorial Fund. As yet no decision had been made for spending the three hundred dollars raised at the alumni dance. "There are only six weeks left of school. Unless we come up with something, we might as well write the whole idea off as a complete flop," Dick said.

"Someone suggested a bronze plaque in the main foyer," Dave Riordan put in.

"Or a bird bath for the center of the quad?" Laurel added.

"A plaque, a bird bath—honestly!" Betty wrinkled her nose. "I mean . . . Gabriel was so young, so talented." Perhaps she had not explained it very well but the others caught her meaning. An impersonal plaque on a stone wall hardly seemed a fitting exchange for a life so young and promising.

"If you're still thinking of something like the Amando Castro Scholarship in Los Angeles, that's out," Dick said. "We don't have enough money. One scholarship and it would be gone."

"Maybe we could buy art books for the library?" As quickly as the words popped out of her mouth, Betty shook her head canceling them. "No good. Mrs. Bellamar gave us an art library when she started the scholarship."

"That's it!" Laurel exulted. "The Wesley T. Bellamar Art Scholarship!"

Bewildered, everyone stared at her. Dave made a small circular motion by his ear, indicating that she had gone slightly daft.

"I mean it!" Laurel insisted, eyes sparkling. "It was ten years ago that Mrs. Bellamar started the scholarship. How many students have won it in ten years? Just two, I think. Practically a straight A average, outstanding art work . . ." Laurel shuddered. "Who's that good? Why half the time no one even applies for it. If we could persuade Mrs. Bellamar to change the four-year scholarship, award it in Gabriel's name to some really deserving Mexican-American student . . . ?"

"Laurel, you're a genius!" Betty jumped up to give the blonde girl a hug and almost knocked her over backward in her chair. The others were laughing now, partly in agreement, partly at Betty's explosive exuberance. Only Dick shook his head. "It's a wonderful idea. But you really don't think we could persuade Mrs. Bellamar to change the scholarship, do you? She may be the richest woman in town, but I bet she hasn't changed one idea or moved one stick of furniture in that mausoleum of hers in thirty years."

Laurel's face sobered. "I know. You practically have to be a descendant of the Pilgrim Fathers with a five-figure bank account to get inside those iron gates. But Dad's a member of the school board, so at least we could talk to her."

"You're right. It's such a good idea, it's worth a try," Dick agreed. "I'll talk to Mr. Huxley and you speak to your father. Maybe we can see her this week . . ."

Before the conversation could continue, it was interrupted by the arrival of Pam and Babs. Face flushed, Pam collapsed into a chair. "This Fiesta—we're going in circles!"

"I told you, you should have gotten into activities before," Betty teased. "By now you'd be used to the confusion."

"Don't pick on Pammy, she's making a darn good co-chairman," Babs laughed. Then with her usual efficiency, she flipped open her notebook. "The *marache* orchestra has been hired. Debate Society is taking the *tacos* booth. Home Econ has *enchiladas*. That still leaves the Girl's League . . ." She paused, looking at Betty. "We'd like to serve some really special Mexican dish. Something entirely different. I thought maybe you could help."

Betty looked down at the table, a puckery crease between her eyes. *Emplanadas?* No, the little meat pies were too much like the *enchiladas* and *tacos* they were serving already. *Pan de dulce?* They had already decided on *tortillas.* Then her head popped up. "*Pipián.*"

"*Pipián?*" everyone echoed.

"It's a traditional holiday dish, a kind of stew made of turkey and spices," Betty explained. "My mother should know the recipe."

"It sounds perfect—and practical too. Turkey goes such a long way." Babs enthusiastically made an entry in her notebook. "We'll count on you for the arrangements."

But Mrs. Ochoa had forgotten the recipe for *pipián.* As she stood at the stove deftly browning a pot roast which was neither very special nor very Mexican, her dark brows tilted worriedly. "It has been so long . . . Grandmother Ortega would know, only she is visiting Aunt Rosa in Laredo." Then as she popped a lid over the roast, her face brightened. "I have it. Josephina Flores. Mrs. Flores will know the recipe."

Before Betty could form the question, her mother nodded. "Run along with you. We will not eat until seven."

It was the first time that Betty had been to Pete's house. A block before she reached El Tipo Café, she turned off on a narrow street lined with modest frame houses; then onto another, unpaved now, the homes even smaller. But in spite of an occasional sagging porch and peeling paint, all maintained a jaunty air with their bright gardens of geraniums, poppies, and nasturtiums; and here and there sweet-scented honeysuckle tumbling over a picket fence. At the last house, smaller than the rest but brightened by a row of blooming cactus in coffee-can containers on the porch, Betty recognized Pete lounging on the steps.

Like two black wings, his brows drew together. But beneath the familiar scowl Betty caught a twinkle of amusement. "Hi. You came a long way just to see me."

Mustering as much dignity as was possible with flaming cheeks, Betty fumbled with the catch on the gate. "I didn't come to see you, Mr. Conceited! I came to see your mother."

Pete shrugged. Rising lazily, he disappeared into the house. "Well, really!" Betty fumed as she looked at the rudely closed door. But minutes later it opened again, revealing Mrs. Flores' friendly brown face. Smiling and nodding, she ushered Betty inside as though she were a very grand lady.

The room was much smaller than Betty's living room at home, and it obviously doubled as sleeping quarters for part of the family. But everything was as immaculate as though it had been freshly dusted only seconds before. In one corner was a television set, almost painful in its contrasting newness; on the wall the familiar shrine of Our Lady of Guadalupe. But as Mrs. Flores hastily pulled forward a chair, Betty had already caught a spine-tingling aroma.

"You were preparing dinner. Can't we talk in the kitchen?" she asked.

Beaming at such a display of informality, Mrs. Flores led the way into the next room. Once again she went through the ceremony of dusting off an already spotless chair. By now Betty had traced the enticing odor to a huge iron pot on the back of the stove. If Mrs. Flores could make *pipián* just half as well as her everyday chili beans, the success of the Girl's League booth was assured!

It took only a minute to explain her errand. She told Mrs. Flores about the Fiesta and how the Girl's League wanted a very special dish. "My mother says you make the very best *pipián*."

Pete lounged in the doorway, scowling more darkly than ever. "My mother doesn't have to work for anyone," he interrupted.

It was the final straw. "I'm not asking her to work for anyone." Betty shot Pete such a withering look that even he looked startled. With a smile she returned to Mrs. Flores. "We're asking you to be in charge of the booth, Mrs. Flores. All you have to do is give the orders. My mother, Mrs. Sutherland, and some other women will do the work."

Out of the corner of her eye, Betty saw that the belligerence had drained from Pete's face. Now it was Mrs. Flores' turn to be hesitant. "I really don't know . . ."

"Of course you'll do it, Mother. You'll help them." Pete was actually grinning.

"Pete's right. Please, Mrs. Flores." Betty entreated. "My mother will be right here too. In fact, she's having the ladies over to our house tomorrow, just so you can meet them." The last was an outright lie, but Betty seized on it as sheer inspiration. Besides, she was certain her mother would agree to the arrangement.

"Well." Mrs. Flores' faced expanded into a proud smile. "*Sí, sí*, it will give me much pleasure."

Betty forgot her anger of a moment before as she and Pete exchanged a victorious wink. Her errand with Mrs. Flores had been completed, but she knew it would be the height of rudeness to depart so quickly. While Mrs. Flores made a pot of coffee, they discussed their families, Father Gargan, and the church. When Betty finally rose to leave, the first long shadows traced a pattern on the street outside. "It is late. Pete must walk with you part of the way," Mrs. Flores insisted.

Six o'clock on a May evening could hardly be called late, but Pete had already snatched his leather jacket from a chair. As the two of them closed the wicket gate and started up the dusty street, Betty was aware of the curious stares of the children playing in the roadway, of the groups of men, tired from a day's work, lounging on the small porches. From one of the houses came the sound of a radio playing a plaintive Spanish melody. Pete moved closer, his arm brushing hers. "Tomorrow everyone will be saying you are my girl."

Betty wished she didn't flush so easily. Suddenly she was remembering the Christmas party and that sprig of mistletoe. "Just because we are walking together?" she murmured.

"Sure." Pete grinned down at the small, dark head, barely reaching his shoulder. "Remember you're across the tracks now. Down here a man doesn't walk his girl in the evening unless he means it."

Betty knew Pete was teasing—partly. She didn't mind the teasing; it was the other, that unknown part, that bothered her. She remembered Dr. Jim's warning. "Across the tracks!" she sniffed, pretending to be angry. "There you go again. You know there are just as many Mexican families on the other side of Meridian Avenue!"

But for once Pete refused to rise to the bait. He shrugged. "Maybe. But it still means the same thing."

From somewhere a sudden chill evening breeze ruffled the dust of the street and Betty shivered. Before she could protest, Pete slipped out of his jacket and draped it around her shoulders. Betty had to admit the jacket felt good, the fleece lining still warm from the heat of Pete's body. Suddenly something like a small giggle rose in her throat. What would her Northridge friends say if they could see her now? Walking along the street with Pete Flores and wearing a *Los Coyotes* jacket! But it was even more surprising to discover that the thought did not bother her particularly.

"I hear you're quite a ball player, Pete. Dick says you're the best pitcher we have this year." Betty jockeyed the conversation to safer ground.

"Oh, I guess I'm okay," Pete admitted with unusual modesty for him. Then his dark eyes swung to her sharply. "You haven't been coming to any of the games."

"I'm pretty busy."

Pete stopped; his hands grasped her arms. "We're playing a home game Friday. Why don't you come then?"

Betty looked down at his muscular hands, detaining her so easily yet so securely. It was a disturbing sensation: vague uneasiness mixed with secret pleasure. It was hardly the same as that invitation to the dance. A baseball game was quite different. "Maybe I will come," Betty told him. "I'd like to see you play."

Pete's teeth flashed in that white, even grin. "That's a promise. I'll be watching for you." He still made no movement to release her arms. If anything, his grip tightened so that the two of them were standing closer together. "Remembering the Christmas party? I've been thinking . . . I thought maybe . . ."

Betty looked away quickly, not trusting herself to meet his dark eyes. It was back again, that dangerous quicksand of Dr. Jim's warning: *Unless you're willing to accept Pete just as he is.* Then almost bursting with relief, she spotted a familiar figure turning onto Meridian Avenue ahead of them. "Carmen! Carmen wait for us!" she called.

If Pete did not like the idea of the sudden threesome, it was too late to do anything about it. Carmen was already waiting to join them.

"Am I glad to find you," she greeted Betty excitedly. Under one arm she carried a Manila art folder. "I wanted to ask you about my entry for the contest. What kind of picture does it have to be?"

"Any kind—oils, tempera, water colors," Betty explained. Then remembering Carmen's vigorous, primitive style, her vivid choice of colors, Betty smiled. "Try to make it simple, Carmen. Just paint something simple and beautiful, something you really love."

At the corner of Paloma Road, Betty said good-by to Carmen and Pete. As she returned Pete's leather jacket, once again she thought she saw that amused twinkle in his eyes. But hurrying down the street minutes later, she was not occupied with thoughts of Pete Flores. The art contest! How could she have forgotten? There was only one week left and she hadn't even started her own entry.

18

The Biggest Dragon

Friday morning dawned bright and honey-scented with the promise of summer, which lay just around the corner. On the steps of Bellamar High, girls in gay summer dresses, boys in gaudy sport shirts competed with the stiff-necked zinnias that lined the walks in their display of vivid colors. Betty waltzed up the steps, a lilt in her footsteps and a song in her heart. A day like this could have been created only for something very special.

But one look at Laurel and Dick waiting for her outside Mr. Huxley's office and the song turned to a dirge. Their long faces made little need for the question already rising to her lips. "No, we didn't get the scholarship." Dick's face was a black thunderhead. "I told you it wouldn't be any use. That woman's not just fifty years behind in her thinking—she's positively medieval!"

"Oh, Mrs. Bellamar wasn't that bad," Laurel soothed. "It seems she just isn't interested in offering a scholarship to students of Mexican parentage. She claims they'll only get menial jobs anyway, and it would be a waste of money. But she did promise to think it over."

"Think it over!" Dick parroted. "We have to make a decision now."

"Well, the memorial dance was your idea," Laurel pouted. "Now it's up to you to come up with something brilliant."

Dick's head lifted. "I have come up with something brilliant. Betty, why don't you go to see Mrs. Bellamar?"

"Me?" Betty's eyes widened.

"Yes, you," Dick insisted with his usual bluntness. "You're a whiz at talking people into things. And you're of what Mrs. Bellamar so delicately calls 'Latin parentage.' Maybe if she saw that you didn't go around in a *Los Coyotes* jacket, with a rose in your teeth and doing a hat dance, she might get rid of some of her stupid prejudice."

For a second Betty stifled a laugh as her mind flew back to last Monday, walking along Meridian Avenue with Pete's big jacket on her shoulders. If Dick only knew! But the subject was too serious for amusement to remain. Besides, another painful memory was crowding in.

"No, thanks. Count me out," she replied.

"Why?" Dick persisted. "I still think you could put it over."

Betty stared down at the tips of her white flats. She couldn't tell Dick that she was thinking of his mother, remembering a pair of cold, unwelcoming eyes and frosted fingertips. No, she wasn't ever going through that again!

"It just wouldn't work. Mrs. Bellamar is still living forty years ago, when Bellamar was all citrus groves and the Mexican *braceros* lived in their own little *colonia* across the tracks. She won't admit that there's a whole new generation now who are American citizens." Then trying not to notice the disappointment in Dick's eyes, she added hastily. "Besides, I haven't the time. I have to work on my entry for the art contest."

"Sure, Betty, I understand." Then as the warning bell sounded, Dick grimaced and shifted the books under his arm. "Well, I guess we're back to the plaque or the bird bath."

That afternoon, by the time Betty got away after a last-minute word with Miss Potter, the baseball game was already under way. For a moment Betty had been tempted to forget the game. Miss Potter had filled her with such enthusiasm that she wanted to rush home and start on her entry immediately. But a promise is a promise, and a prick of loyalty turned her steps from the beckoning front walk, across the grass to the playing field.

Baseball did not draw the crowds that attended the football games. Even this spring, with their first winning team in nearly five years, the bleachers were only a quarter full. Tyler High, champions for the last two years, had a bigger attendance in their stands across the way. Betty saw Dick. But he was busy talking to Morrie and Dave, so she slipped into a front row seat next to some girls from Beaux Arts.

It was the third inning, the game still scoreless. Pete, muscular and relaxed, stood on the mound for Bellamar. The afternoon was humid. Already Pete's white shirt clung damply to his broad shoulders and along one hip was a grimy marking of dust and resin where he had wiped his hand. But as he sent that fast ball sizzling across the plate, then a change-of-pace curve that caught the batters unaware, Betty realized that he was really good. Already there were grumblings from the stands across the way.

At least Bellamar had put three men on base, though they had failed to score. But as yet Pete had refused to give up a single hit. In the seventh inning, when Bellamar's first baseman streaked across home plate on a long double by Owen Westbrook, the stands went wild. The eighth inning again was scoreless. Then it was that crucial top half of the ninth with Tyler at bat, and Pete was trying to bring home the victory, a no-hitter.

The loss of the game would mean the loss of the championship for Tyler. As Pete fanned the first batter, the grumblings and catcalls increased. It wasn't good-natured jeering now—suddenly it had become spiteful and ugly.

"Where'd you get that Mexican pitcher?"

"What makes you think you can pitch . . . Greaser!"

Betty saw the dark color stain Pete's face. Rattled by the taunts, he let two high balls escape him.

"I told you he was no good!" someone jeered exultantly.

"Why don't you go back to Mexico?"

Pete swung around furiously, dropping the ball, his fists knotted. Betty froze to her seat. She knew Pete's violent temper. They had him rattled and raging now. He would throw the whole game.

"Throw out the Spic! Throw out the Spic!" came the goading chant from across the way.

It was the worst demonstration of poor sportsmanship Betty had ever seen. She jumped to her feet. "Come on, Pete! Come on, you can do it. Don't listen to them, Pete!" As though on a signal, the others around her rose, their cheers drowning the rooters across the way.

Abruptly Pete turned and picked up the resin bag. The next ball came straight and true, so swift that the swinging batter never touched it. "Come on, Pete! *Vaya*! *Vaya*!" Betty shrieked. In her excitement she hardly noticed she had lapsed into Spanish. She continued to shout until Pete had put down the final batter and, as with one voice, the cheer of victory rose from the Bellamar stands.

Already rooters were spilling onto the fields. Betty recognized the rough, loud-talking boys who had led the Tyler hecklers. Pete had seen them too. Fists doubling again, he lunged forward. But Owen and several of his teammates were too quick for him. Before trouble could start, they had swung Pete to their shoulders and were carrying him off the field. It was impossible to reach him through the press of the crowd. But for just a moment before Pete's head dipped out of sight through the locker-room doorway, he looked back. His eyes met Betty's and he flashed her a grin that was happy, triumphant, and very tired.

Betty was glad that she had come to the game. That look in Pete's eyes had told her he was glad too. It was more than just the victory over Tyler for Pete this afternoon. Out there on the mound he had won an even greater victory over himself and his own violent, unpredictable temper.

Suddenly, through that swelling pride in Pete's achievement, Betty was aware of a stab of guilt. If he had conquered his private dragon, wasn't it time she started conquering some dragons too? If for the good of Bellamar, Pete had found the courage to face three hundred heckling rooters, couldn't she face just one woman?

Spotting Dick in the crowd, Betty hurried to catch him. "Dick, I've changed my mind," she blurted. "I will go to see Mrs. Bellamar."

The following afternoon, dressed in a crisp yellow linen

suit, smart white cloche and matching gloves, which had been her Easter present from her parents, Betty walked up exclusive Ridge Road. If Dick's home with its white colonnade had seemed like a mansion, it was dwarfed by the Bellamar estate a block further up the street. A three-storied sprawling, museum piece of slate-colored stone, ornate with jutting spires and cupolas, the Bellamar mansion had been the town showplace for years. Secretly Betty considered it an architectural monstrosity; but since the original Wesley Bellamar had planted his first navel oranges and built this monument to his harvest of gold, no one had dared make the observation. Betty was thankful the iron gates were open. If they had been closed she wouldn't have had the slightest idea of what to do.

An elderly maid in a rustling uniform answered the bell. Betty swallowed the lump in her throat. "I'm Miss Ochoa. I believe Mrs. Bellamar is expecting me?"

Inside, she waited in a huge hallway while the maid disappeared down a smaller, paneled hall to the right. Betty was not certain whether to sit in one of the uncomfortable-looking, high-backed chairs or remain standing beside a pedestal with a marble bust of the late Mr. Bellamar. She decided on the latter. After an interminable interval, during which she was quite certain she had been forgotten, she finally heard voices.

An imposing, eagle-faced woman with iron-gray hair done in a mountainous coil on top of her head bore down upon her. "Oh yes, Miss Ochoa." It was hardly a handshake. Mrs. Bellamar's hand withdrew so quickly, it barely grazed Betty's fingertips.

She led the way down the hall. "Mr. Huxley told me you were coming. I'm afraid I can tell you right now though, you're wasting your time."

Seated in the library, a dark room filled with hundreds of books looking musty and forgotten behind their glass-faced coffins, Betty found that her carefully rehearsed speech had all but vanished. "I'm sorry if you think I'm wasting your time, Mrs. Bellamar," she began politely. "But I don't feel I'm wasting mine. In fact, that is one of the reasons why I am here . . . I think the people of Bellamar have wasted too much time already."

Even to Betty's ears it sounded like an auspicious beginning. Suddenly she had regained her composure and her memory. She proceeded with her speech. When she had concluded, there was no trace of emotion on Mrs. Bellamar's face.

"Of course, you understand I have nothing against persons of Mexican parentage. After all, my family and Mr. Bellamar's family hired Mexican laborers in their groves for years." Betty was rewarded with the barest flicker of a smile. "But honestly, Miss Ochoa, just between the two of us: how many of those children from Meridian Avenue would benefit by such a scholarship? The majority have no ambition whatsoever; they are content to remain laborers, you know that."

"I don't know any such thing," Betty protested almost rudely. "Maybe that was true years ago. But the groves are gone now. Many of the Mexican-Americans are veterans. They own their own homes. They work in stores, factories, offices. They have the same ambitions as everyone else."

"But why the Wesley T. Bellamar Scholarship—why my scholarship?" Mrs. Bellamar insisted.

"Because we couldn't raise enough money alone. Because the Bellamar Scholarship is the least useful . . ." Betty stopped abruptly, face coloring, as she realized how impolite this must sound. She hastily corrected herself. "I mean it's really a fine scholarship, Mrs. Bellamar. But the conditions are so difficult—an A average, outstanding talent in art. Why, students who can meet those requirements don't really need your scholarship. This year no one is even trying for it."

"Gabriel Delgado won the scholarship and he was of Latin parentage. If these other students want scholarships so badly, let them meet the requirements as Gabriel did!" Mrs. Bellamar's eyes flashed. It was obvious that she was not accustomed to being opposed, at least, not by a slip of a girl.

But Betty forgot caution as she warmed to a favorite subject. Already she was envisioning the young people of Meridian Avenue, Benny, Pete, Carmen, making wonderful successes in life. "But Gabriel was a genius!" she exploded. "He didn't need your scholarship. It isn't always the brilliant student who needs the most help; he can take care of himself. The Delgado scholarship could mean the books and tuition to help some earnest student to go on to college. It could mean an entire course in trade school for some boy with mechanical ability, a secretarial course for a girl with a large family of brothers and sisters to help support. It wouldn't have to be a brilliant student—just some hard-working student who had proven his determination to better himself in life."

For a second Betty thought she saw a splinter of interest in Mrs. Bellamar's eyes. Then the icy veil returned and the older woman looked bored. "I can see you are a very earnest young woman and I admire your spirit. But I really do not have time to discuss the matter further. Later, if I should change my mind, I can call you." The tone of Mrs. Bellamar's voice left no doubt that the subject was closed and

Betty was being dismissed. As if by magic, the elderly maid had reappeared to show her to the door.

As Betty rose from the chair, she felt Mrs. Bellamar's eyes appraising her: the well-tailored suit, the spotless gloves. "Ochoa . . . ?" she mused softly. "That sounds like a Spanish name. You must come from one of the old Spanish families?"

Two spots of color fanned Betty's cheeks. "Not Spanish," she replied hotly, "just plain, old, third-generation Mexican!" Then with as much dignity as remained, she followed the maid down the hall to the door.

If the walk up the long drive had seemed endless, the retreat seemed even farther, so great was Betty's desire to escape. Safely outside the iron gates, unmindful of her clean suit, she sank to the curbstone. What a horrible, prejudiced old woman! What a hideous, musty old house! The idea of calling her Spanish . . . as though being Mexican was something to be hidden!

Suddenly Betty knew how Pete felt. That feeling that came from being struck where it hurt most, in the deep, secret pride of your own heart. That feeling that came from being helpless to strike back. At least Pete could work out his resentment in a flailing street fight!

Betty's only recourse was to bend down, pick up a small rock, and with grim satisfaction, send it clattering against the iron gate. Then looking around to make certain no one had seen such a display, she primly dusted her gloves and continued down the street.

19

Look Who Won!

Betty wasn't satisfied with the painting. She had decided on a water color of the cliffs at Laguna because it had been another seascape which had taken third place last year. She had stayed up late, darkening a shadow here, straightening a line there; but in the bright morning sunlight she recognized that the painting, though pleasant enough, still lacked that certain flair. She had waited too long and hurried too fast. As she recalled her enthusiasm of last fall, her plans to come up with a contest winner, the disappointment was unbearable.

"What a long face! You look like a balloon that has been pricked," her mother teased as Betty slumped into her chair at the breakfast table with an audible sigh.

"That's exactly how I feel," Betty agreed morosely. "My painting isn't any good. My grades are only mediocre. In a few weeks I will be graduating and I haven't accomplished one thing this year to make you proud of me."

Mrs. Ochoa threw back her head, her laughter filling the sunny kitchen. "Graduation blues! I think every senior has them. You wait, the Fiesta on Thursday will bring you out of it."

But as Betty continued to stare at her plate, without a vestige of reciprocating smile, Mrs. Ochoa bent to drop a kiss on the small, dark head. "Well, I am proud of you—very proud. Good grades, doing big things, they aren't everything. Doing your best, doing those things which are right for you to do, that is what counts. Your father and I had a long talk last night. It is a little hard right now, with Gloria's music lessons, Larry's teeth needing straightening—but you must not worry. I think we can manage a little money toward college this fall."

"Oh, Mamma!" Betty spun around to catch her mother in a breathless hug. "You—you're the most! I could find a part-time job to earn the rest."

But later, as she wrapped the water color to take to school, even her mother's good news that they would be able to help her go to college did not bring the anticipated joy. She thought of how she had neglected her family this last year, the many times her mother and Gloria had taken over her household chores because she had been busy at school. Somehow the thought of their sacrificing even more was not a satisfying one. If only she could have accomplished one thing that was really outstanding!

Miss Potter was disappointed with the painting. "Yes, Betty, it is nice—it's very much like the one you painted last year, isn't it?" Of course, she was too considerate to say more, but Betty could read it in her eyes. For four years Betty had been one of Miss Potter's favorite pupils; she had expected her to come up with something much better. As Betty left the art room, she told herself that there was no need to use the stairs. She was only surprised that leaden weight wasn't sufficient to plummet her right through the three floors to her locker in the basement.

But Mrs. Ochoa had been right. Gloomy thoughts, graduation blues, had no place at the Fiesta. Thursday came in a diamond day; starting with the fresh dew sparkling on the grass, and ending with even the gray walls glistening under their riotous banners and festoons calling the visitors to take part in the Fiesta inside. Morning classes were disrupted, half the students out on special pass to put the finishing touches to the booths. At noon all pretense was discarded and early dismissal marked the start of the festivities.

For the first two hours Betty worked in the Spanish Club concession, serving hot tamales to a long line of impatient customers. At three o'clock, when she was finally relieved, she was glad to escape from the steaming booth. Buying one of the tamales for herself and wrapping it carefully in a napkin, she headed into the crowd.

There was no doubt that the Fiesta was a success. Everywhere there were happy faces. Besides the students, there were many townspeople and it looked as if almost all of Meridian Avenue was there. Babs and Laurel hurried by, faces flushed and laughing under two of the huge, fringed straw hats being sold at one of the booths. Behind them came three small, olive-skinned girls in authentic Mexican costumes.

"Hey, wait a minute!" A hand stopped Betty so abruptly she choked on the last bite of tamale. As she spun around her nose grazed a gaily embroidered vest. It was Dick. With his fancy vest and black sombrero he made a handsome vaquero—except possibly for his ash-blond hair.

"I've been chasing you all the way from the tamale booth." He pretended to be gasping for air. "I have something to tell you."

A moment later they had edged out of the crowd and found a quiet spot between two booths. "I don't know how important this is," Dick began, the tone of his voice betraying that he thought it was quite important, "but guess who I saw this morning?"

"Who? I can't possibly guess." Betty's voice bounced with impatience.

"Mrs. Bellamar," Dick announced dramatically. "Mrs. Wesley T. Bellamar. A big chauffeured limousine stopped out in front this morning, and no one less than the *grande dame* herself sailed into Mr. Huxley's office."

"You don't think . . . you don't really believe . . . ?" Betty's voice came wonderingly.

"Well, I don't really know anything yet," Dick admitted. "But why would she be coming down here unless it was about the scholarship? Maybe she changed her mind. Maybe you did as good a selling job on her as you did on Mrs. Moreno and Mrs. Flores."

"I hardly think so." Betty shook her head, remembering that unpleasant interview. Then, not wanting to spoil Dick's hopes, she flashed him her sunny smile. "But we can always dream, can't we?"

As they joined the crowd, she stared about her with a vague, happy smile. "That's it!" she announced suddenly.

"That's what?" Dick asked curiously.

Betty tossed him an impish smile. "That's what I'll be

when I get out of school. I've been worrying about it all week. I'll become a super-saleslady."

"Heaven forbid!" Dick struck his forehead in imaginary panic. "Everyone'll buy more than they can afford. Financial ruin for the nation. You'll be the only one left with any money."

That was part of the fun of being with Dick, their silly crossfire of banter. "That's suits me," Betty tossed her head. "Then when I have all the money, I'll start a thousand Gabriel Delgado scholarships."

But their joking couldn't continue forever, not with the Fiesta crying for attention. Dick waved good-by as he spotted some friends; moments later Betty found Agnes and Pam. For the next few hours they made the rounds of the booths, stuffing themselves with popcorn and *enchiladas*, trying their luck at the various games. Then it was almost five o'clock and time for Betty to relieve the girls at the art booth. Waving good-by, she started through the crowd.

The Beaux Arts booth was set a little apart from the others at the edge of the quad. Here in the long corridor between the Science wing and the auditorium, the easels had been set up with the contest entries. Betty wondered if she had been purposely avoiding this side of the quad, avoiding this moment. By now the prizes would have been awarded.

The art display always drew a good crowd, and the corridor was jammed with visitors. Betty found her water color between a charcoal drawing of a horse and a still life of a bowl of fruit. There was no prize. "That's rather pretty," a woman was commenting as she passed. Betty was thankful for the compliment, but it still couldn't erase her disappointment. Not even an honorable mention, and they gave six of those!

Where the largest crowd was gathered midway down the aisle, Betty knew by instinct she would find the first-prize winner. It took a moment for her to elbow into a position of advantage. It was a bold, vigorous portrait in tempera. The style was almost primitive, but as Betty looked at the dazzling robe in ochres and greens, the dusky mantle of gold, the simple brown face with the lustrous eyes that were at the same time challenging yet infinitely sad, she realized that this picture had caught it—that spark of imagination she had tried so hard to achieve. At the bottom hung the blue first-prize ribbon: "Our Blessed Lady of Guadalupe" by Carmen Ortiz.

Betty felt a swelling lump in her throat. Carmen had won first place . . . her Carmen! She hardly realized she had used the possessive as she remembered Carmen's asking her advice about the entry. She had told her to paint something simple and beautiful that she loved. What could be more beautiful or dearly loved by Carmen than Our Lady of Guadalupe, the patroness saint of the Mexican people—the same little brown lady who had her place in every good Mexican home? Before the lump could dissolve completely into a misty feeling in her eyes, Betty slipped back into the crowd. If she could not win the contest herself, there was no one she would rather win it than Carmen.

Much later Betty sat in the art booth with two other girls. It was beginning to get dark now. Already some of the booths were closing, out of food, silly straw hats, and prizes for the games. The crowd was thinning, drifting toward the gymnasium where the dance would continue for another hour yet. Besides the drawing card of the contest, Beaux Arts had sold fifteen paintings, which was a good average considering that few people came to a Fiesta planning to take home a water color or an oil painting.

As Betty sat staring into space, someone jostled her elbow. "I'd like to buy a picture . . . that little water color over there of Laguna."

Why, it was hers. . . . Startled, Betty looked up into her father's smiling face. "Oh, Father, you're teasing!" she laughed.

"I certainly am *not* teasing." Mr. Ochoa's smile included the two other girls. "I intend to buy that painting. It's just what I want to hang in my den."

What a wonderful father she had, Betty thought as she wrapped the picture for a second time. At least her painting would not be one of those left over to be handed out and returned in art class. At least her painting would be among those that had sold.

"I didn't expect you to come," she told her father.

"And miss a fiesta?" Mr. Ochoa's jovial voice made light of the tired lines around his eyes. Then he added more soberly, "Your mother is almost through now. I think perhaps we should go home. You both must be very tired."

"Miss Ochoa tired?" a hearty voice interrupted them. "That I have to see!" It was Dr. Jim; close on his heels came Pete.

Before Betty could fumble with introductions, Dr. Jim was pumping her father's hand. "How's that boy of yours? Fallen out of any more apricot trees?" Of course her father knew Dr. Jim—he had set Larry's arm. But what about Pete?

"*Hola,*" he saluted with a faint return of his old bravado.

Betty felt a sudden coldness in her chest. Suddenly she knew this was a moment she had been dreading. It wasn't just her Anglo friends who were prejudiced; there was prejudice among her own people too, prejudice between those who had come farther along the road of Americanism and those who were just starting out. She had been guilty of it herself. She could see it in her father now, the stiffening of his shoulders, that mask of reserve that dropped across his face. If her father thought of Pete at all, it was only as the angry voice on their front porch one night, as the boy who brought heartache to his mother and a bad reputation to all the Mexican people by his wild escapades. "But, Papa, Pete isn't like that really!" Betty wanted to cry out to him. "He isn't what you are thinking."

Then Dr. Jim stepped into the painful gap; his arm around Pete's shoulders. "Mr. Ochoa, you remember Pete Flores, don't you? He's one of my best boys down at the Center . . . an up-and-coming boxer too. You ought to come down some night and see our bouts. Father Gargan is a regular fan."

Slowly, somewhat cautiously, the reserve dropped from Mr. Ochoa's face. He extended his hand. "I'm glad to see you again, Pete."

There was no longer any need for Betty to remain at the booth. When they reached the *pipián* booth, they found that it, too, was closed and Betty's mother and Mrs. Flores waiting. "We might as well give Mrs. Flores and Pete a ride home in our car," Mr. Ochoa said, taking charge of the situation. From the direction of the gym came the enticing beat of a rumba.

"But the dance is going to last for another hour!" Pete blurted.

"I'm really not tired at all," Betty protested.

Once again Mr. Ochoa's eyes had that guarded look. Dr. Jim glanced at his watch. "I don't have to be back to the clinic until eight o'clock. Why don't you let the young people stay? I'll drive them home." It was too late for Mr. Ochoa to protest. What could he say with his wife already nodding eagerly and Mrs. Flores standing so close at her side?

"It's a pretty good dance." Pete made an awkward stab at conversation. "I hear *Los Hildagos* are planning some dances for this summer too." Betty nodded agreement, feet and body hypnotized by the rhythm of the music. She smiled across the room at Dr. Jim, dancing with Carla Delgado. It was true there had been a number of surprised faces when she had stepped onto the floor with Pete Flores. But somehow there had not been as many shocked looks as she had anticipated.

She glanced up into the heavy-lashed black eyes that could be so warm and teasing when they were not clouded with anger. It could hardly be called a real date—just an hour at a carnival dance. Maybe it would never reach the stage of a real date; there were still many barriers—just how many she had realized for the first time today. Some of those barriers had been in her own heart. But she and Pete had come a long way these last months; both of them had changed. But of one thing she was very sure: as soon as school was out this summer, she was going to join *Los Hildagos*!

20

Tomorrow's Children

The entire senior class seemed to fill the quad with a milling sea of gray graduation robes. As they straggled into place in the two lines that would enter the auditorium, some were laughing and tilting their strange, new mortarboards at rakish angles; others, more pensive, were trying to swallow a sudden thickening in their throats. Betty found that she belonged to the latter group. It was an exciting yet sad feeling. Three more days and they would be going up these same steps for graduation itself. But today was equally solemn. For this was the final-awards assembly, the last time they would sit with their other classmates as an entire student body. Four long years they had worked, studied, and played together. Now, it was almost over.

The lines had formed now; inside, the school orchestra struck the notes of the processional. As the seniors dipped into the shadowed dimness of the auditorium and began their slow march down the aisles, the faces of the lower classmen already seated at the rear turned to watch them. As Betty passed the junior section a warm, brown hand shot out to seize hers in a brief squeeze. It was Carmen. Betty tossed her a quick smile. Already she had heard the good news. Carmen, who would not be graduating for another year, had been elected the new secretary of Beaux Arts.

Then the long march was completed. Mr. Vernon, the orchestra leader, lowered his arms and with a rustling of robes the seniors took their seats in the front.

First came the formal business of the assembly, with Dick turning his gavel over to chunky junior, Walt Ivers, who would be the new student body president. The new officers seated, Coach Walters stepped forward to begin the athletic awards. As Pete Flores, face ruddy with a proud kind of embarrassment, went forward to receive a baseball letter and lifetime pass to all of the Bellamar games, Betty realized with a little stab in her heart that it was the first time in Pete's life he had received public recognition for something outstanding. Following the athletic awards came others for special achievements.

Finally a long pause settled over the auditorium. This was the moment all had been anticipating, the moment when the "most outstanding senior" would be named. As Mr. Huxley stepped forward to make the presentation, Betty's heart hovered in her throat.

"I don't believe I really need to tell you the winner of this year's award." The principal smiled at the audience.

"For four years of outstanding scholarship, notable athletic achievement, continuous student leadership, and service to those highest principles for which our school stands, I give you Bellamar High School's most outstanding senior . . . your former student body president . . . Richard Paul Ackerman."

The auditorium swelled with applause. As Betty watched Dick stride across the stage to receive the award, she realized that all her jealousy was gone and she was clapping louder than all the others. Dick was the one who deserved the award. Whatever good they had accomplished, it had been Dick who had sparked and led them all.

When Dick had returned to his seat on the stage, the final portion of the assembly began, the awarding of scholarships. Roger Eaton won the Science Scholarship; a tall, jolly-looking girl, the Home Economics Fellowship. Several other scholarships to individual colleges were presented. A few more minutes and it would be over; they would rise to sing the alma mater for the last time.

As though he had been saving this for the very last, Mr. Huxley stepped forward. "We have one more scholarship— a scholarship which it gives me great pleasure to announce is being awarded this year for the first time. I have two reasons for being proud of this scholarship. One, because it has been given in loving memory of a fine and talented young man. Two, because you, the students of Bellamar, through your enthusiasm, your donations, and your determination, are largely responsible for the creation of this award. For the funds to make it a permanent, four-year scholarship, we must thank, as always, our perpetual benefactress, Mrs. Wesley T. Bellamar. Beginning this year and continuing every year hereafter, I announce the Gabriel Delgado Memorial Scholarship of three hundred dollars a year, to be presented annually to Bellamar High School's most outstanding student of Mexican-American heritage, to be used for further education in the field of his or her choice."

As the auditorium filled with tumultuous applause, Betty sat too stunned to even clap her hands. They had won! Mrs. Bellamar had supported the scholarship after all! She wanted to pinch herself to make sure this wasn't a dream.

Then Mr. Huxley raised his hands and motioned for silence. "A special board of five members was selected to choose this year's winner. Then Monday morning of this week Mrs. Bellamar herself phoned me. Since it is her financial support that is making possible the continuing nature of this scholarship, she asked if this first year we would give consideration to a candidate she herself had selected." Mr. Huxley paused; his eyes seemed to twinkle. "Oddly enough, by some very strange coincidence, the candidate selected by Mrs. Bellamar happened to be exactly the same one already chosen by unanimous vote of the selection board. For untiring work, for unflagging enthusiasm, for the finest qualities of American citizenship as well as those additional qualities of a fine and proud national culture that has contributed so much to our California way of life, I am proud to present the first Gabriel Delgado Scholarship to Bellamar's most outstanding student of Mexican heritage . . . Elizabeth Mercedes Ochoa."

With a little gasp Betty looked around her. That was she! But she wasn't . . . she didn't. . . . Then laughing friends were pushing her to her feet and she was squeezing through to the aisle. It was only a few rows to the stage, yet as she walked those few feet it seemed that a thousand thoughts were crowding her mind. Was it possible that she was the same girl who had sat in this auditorium nine months ago for a nominating assembly, ashamed of her name, ashamed of her heritage? Now her head was high, two bright spots of color burned in her cheeks. Today she was proud—proud of being American, and Mexican too!

Five minutes later as the final chords of the alma mater faded away, the students began to file out of the auditorium. Betty wasn't the only one dabbing at her eyes. Only she still didn't know what those silly tears were for—sadness that school days were over or this great, bursting happiness inside her.

"Congratulations, Betty!" That was Dick, winking at her over the heads of the others. He must have known about the scholarship all along. That was why he had seemed to be avoiding her this last week, neatly side-stepping any questions about the memorial fund!

"Good work, Betty!" That was Laurel giving her shoulder a brief squeeze. Congratulations. More congratulations . . . Babs, Bill, Dave, Morrie.

But when Betty finally made her way outside into the bright sunlight, it was Agnes and Pam who were waiting, as they always had waited, to walk with her to their next class. For a moment the three of them stood on the steps, watching the students spill past them, streaming across the quad and into the buildings—blonde heads, brunette heads, crew cuts, flattops, duck tails and pompadours. "We really didn't solve anything big," Betty found herself thinking. "Next year there will be a new crop of *pachucos* at Bellamar, new students from exclusive Northridge and middle-class Hawes Street. They'll have their troubles, their animosities too. They'll have to solve their own problems. But at least we have given them a start."

Agnes pinched Betty's arm. "What are you going to do with all that loot?"

Pam giggled as she pressed in on the other side. "What a crazy question! She'll go to art school and become a famous artist, of course."

Betty shook her head. "No, I don't think I'll be an artist." She knew now that her artistic talent was only a small one; she'd never be another Gabriel Delgado. If any one of them was to follow in Gabriel's footsteps, it would be Carmen.

"I'm not really sure," Betty paused. "I'll always love art but I think I'd rather be a teacher . . . an art teacher, of course. And it really isn't *that* much money. I'll still have to work part of my way, you know."

"I'm not worried. I have a feeling you'll make it," Agnes laughed fondly.

From somewhere across the campus came the hollow sound of the warning bell. As Betty waved good-by to Agnes and Pam, a familiar, long shadow joined hers on the cement walk. She realized Pete had been waiting all this time to speak to her alone. "Bravo! Bravo!" he added his congratulations. Then his face sobered with just a hint of the old sullen anger. "I suppose now you'll be leaving Bellamar for good."

"Pete Flores . . . how could you say such a thing!" Betty chided. "Bellamar is my home. Even when I'm in college, I'll be coming back on weekends and holidays." Once again her eyes swept the campus: the green lawns, the gray walls that could loom so formidable to a freshman, so dear to a senior. For some reason Dr. Jim slipped into her mind —Dr. Jim who could have set up an exclusive practice across town but had chosen instead to work among his own people. There was a need in Bellamar for teachers too. Betty smiled at Pete. "In fact, someday I hope I'll be coming back for good."